◉ 英语漫话中国文化系列

【英汉对照】

中国传统文化
经典故事100篇

100 Classic Tales of Traditional Chinese Culture

主编译: 任秀桦 Steve P·Chen

编 译: 任秀桦 Steve P·Chen 迟文成 吴秀萍 卢欣 赵静
张楠 刘晓晔 岑继恒 刘璐 刘悦

插 图: 冯旭
英文校对: Ajaree Whaley

大连理工大学出版社

图书在版编目(CIP)数据

中国传统文化经典故事 100 篇:英汉对照/ 任秀桦,
(美)陈朋(Chen, S.P.)主编、译.—大连:大连理工
大学出版社,2007.11 (2008.5 重印)

ISBN 978-7-5611-3790-1

Ⅰ.中… Ⅱ.①任…②陈… Ⅲ.①英语—汉语—对照读
物②故事—作品集—中国 Ⅳ.H319.4:I

中国版本图书馆 CIP 数据核字(2007)第 158952 号

大连理工大学出版社出版

地址:大连市软件园路 80 号 邮政编码:116023
发行:0411-84708842 传真:0411-84701466 邮购:0411-84703636
E-mail:dutp@dutp.cn URL:http://www.dutp.cn
大连图腾彩色印刷有限公司印刷 大连理工大学出版社发行

幅面尺寸:175mm×168mm 印张:15.5 字数:251 千字
附件:光盘一张 印数:6001~11000
2007 年 11 月第 1 版 2008 年 5 月第 2 次印刷

责任编辑:高 颖 责任校对:刘 皎

封面设计:孙宝福

ISBN 978-7-5611-3790-1 定价:30.00 元

Preface

100 Classic Tales of Traditional Chinese Culture consists of three parts, Part I Fables, Part II Legends and Part III Myths, which are matched with vivid illustrations and plain English translations. This illustrated book helps readers of different cultural backgrounds share the essence beauty of the traditional Chinese cultural heritage. The lovely and interesting tales will quench the thirst of foreigners who are interested in traditional Chinese culture, and the Chinese youngsters who enjoy the topic of traditional Chinese culture bilingually.

Ancient Chinese fables often use exaggerated and imaginary means, as well as distinct and lively languages, to convey moral truth and embody the philosophy of life. The outstanding representatives of them are Zhuangzi's fables. Zhuangzi's fables set forth the mystery and deep philosophy of "Non-action" and "Harmony of Human and Nature" in a romantic and exaggerated artistic style, explaining the secret essence of TAO with simple and common stories, which enable people to chew the taste while they gain enlightenment and moral truth. Fables like *A Walk Learner in Handan*, *A Mantis Blocking a Chariot*, *A Sigh of River* and *Zhuangzhou Borrows Grain* have been widely known by almost all Chinese families.

Ancient Chinese legends are extremely rich and plentiful, passed down from generation to generation, regarded as an invaluable treasure among the folk literatures. Chinese legends are based on real Chinese history, and are often characterized by the folk and race. Some famous Chinese legends like *Lady Meng Jiang Wailed at the Great Wall* , *Three Moves by Mencius´ Mother* , *A Willing Victim Letting Himself. Be Caught* , *Bian He´s Jade* and *Shennong Tastes the Medicines* are widely spread in China down the ages.

Ancient Chinese myths often deal with supernatural beings, ancestors, or heroes in remote antiquity, explaining aspects of the natural world or delineating the psychology and customs of the society, such as, *Nv Wa Saves the Sky*, *Kua Fu Chased the Sun*. The protagonists in myths are often described as immortals or half-immortals. Even though there are supernatural facts in myths, the figures, times, and spots of the stories are often true. Of the most favorite myths of love, *Niu Lang and Zhi Nv*, *Lady White Snake* and *Liang Shanbo and Zhu Yingtai* are most treasured by readers domestic and abroad.

Chinese traditional culture, deeply rooted in these tales, is an intangible heritage from our ancestors. It records wide circulation and spectacular phenomena of the traditional culture, and pervades the blood of Chinese all over the world in sense of kindred spirits, conventions and values. *100 Classic Tales of Traditional Chinese Culture* exudes the flavor of the Chinese race, sparkles with their wisdom and reflects the essence beauty and brilliance of Chinese culture. Readers not only read the vivid tales with implied profound traditional Chinese Culture, but also gain the ability of bilingual perception.

Ren Xiuhua
Non-action Study Beijing
Oct10,2007

前　言

　　《中国传统文化经典故事 100 篇》精选了中国古代寓言故事、中国古代民间传说和中国古代神话故事精品 100 篇,配以生动、传神的插图和简明流畅的英文。本书旨在使具有不同语言文化背景的读者共享中国传统文化之美。这本图文并茂的双语经典读本不仅适合对中国传统文化感兴趣的外国人,也适合想对国际友人传播中国传统文化的炎黄子孙阅读赏析。

　　中国古代寓言故事不仅题材丰富、词语洗练、意象生动而且寓意深刻。其中最杰出的代表是庄子寓言故事。庄子将深奥的哲理寄托在故事之中,通过浪漫而夸张的艺术手法,阐述天人合一、自然无为的哲学思想。寓言故事虽浅显易懂却蕴涵深刻,让人读之难忘,嚼之有味。像《邯郸学步》、《螳臂当车》、《望洋兴叹》、《庄周贷粟》等寓言故事已成为妇孺皆知的经典寓言故事。

　　中国古代民间传说是一种口头文学,是中国民间文化重要的组成部分。民间故事以口耳相传的方式在民众中世代传承,绵延不绝。民间故事内容广泛、情节动人,具有鲜明的时代性、地方性和民族性。有些民间故事如《孟姜女哭长城》、《孟母三迁之教》、《姜太公钓鱼》、《卞和泣玉》、《神农尝百草》等在华夏的大地上已然达到家喻户晓的程度。

　　中国古代神话故事描写的时间范围往往是所谓盘古开天辟地的史前时代,神话故事的话题多围绕人与自然之间的关系,如《女娲补天》、《夸父追日》等。神话故事的典型人物往往被描述成神仙或半神仙式的英雄。描写爱情的神话故事虽然是神话传奇,但故事有具体的发生地点和发生年代,故事的主人翁也经常是真实的人物,其中最为著名的爱情故事《牛郎织女》、《白蛇传》和《梁山伯与祝英台》深受中外读者的喜爱。

中国传统文化是我们从先辈传承下来的丰厚的非物质文化遗产，她记录了中华民族和中国文化发生、演化的历史，并作为世代传袭的人文精神、社会习俗、价值观念等精神遗产渗透在每个中国人的血脉之中。本书所选的经典故事从不同的角度将这些文化遗产呈现给读者，使读者体会到中华文化的博大精深，感悟人生的智慧、生命的真谛，同时在领略中国传统文化韵味中提高双语赏读能力。

任秀桦

于北京无为斋

2007 年 10 月 10 日

Contents 目录

PART 1 FABLES
第一部分 成语故事

目录

2

目录 3

目录

4

目录 3

PART II LEGENDS
第二部分 民间传说

PART III MYTHS
第三部分 神话故事

Part 1 Fables

第一部分
成语故事

 A Loss May Turn Out to Be a Gain
塞翁失马

中国传统文化经典故事100篇·英汉对照

〖A Loss May Turn Out to Be a Gain〗

Long, long ago, there lived an old man named Sai Weng. One day he found his horse missing. It was said that the horse was seen running outside the border of the country. Hearing the news, the neighbors came to comfort him for the unfortunate loss. But Sai Weng was unexpectedly calm and said, "It doesn't matter; it may not be a bad event. On the contrary, I think it can be a good one."

sài wēng shī mǎ
塞 翁 失 马

很久很久以前，有一位老人，名叫塞翁。一天，他发现他的马走失了。据说有人看见马跑过了边境。邻居们听到这事，都来安慰他。塞翁却显得非常平静，他对来的人说："没关系，也未见得是一件坏事。相反，还可能是件好事呢！"

One night Sai Weng heard some noises of horses and got up to see. To his surprise, he saw another beautiful horse as well as his own. It was clear that his horse had brought a companion home. Hearing the news, the neighbors all came to say congratulations on his good luck. At the greetings, however, Sai Weng was very calm and thoughtful. He added, "It is true that I got a new horse for nothing, but it is hard to say whether it is good or bad. It may be an unlucky thing."

一天晚上，塞翁听到马叫声便起身看个究竟。令他大吃一惊的是他不但见到了自己的马，还见到了另外一匹骏马。很显然是他的马把自己的伙伴带回了家。邻居们听到消息后，都跑来道喜。然而塞翁在与邻居们寒暄时显得不仅平静而且若有所思。他说："我是白得了一匹马，不过还很难说这是福还是祸。没准儿是不祥之物。"

Who can expect what he said was found to be right. The son of Sai Weng was very fond of the horse brought home, and one day, when he was riding the horse, he fell off the horse and terribly hurt his left leg. From then on he was never able to walk freely as he used to be. "Nothing serious," Sai Weng said, "perhaps it is going to be good."

A year later, many of the youth there were recruited to fight in a war and most of them died. The son of Sai Weng was absolved from the obligation for his disability, so he escaped death.

谁想到塞翁竟一语成谶。他的儿子特别喜欢那匹骏马。一天他骑马时，不慎从马背上摔落下来，摔断了左腿。从此，他再也不能像从前那样自由行走了。对此，塞翁却说："不碍事，没准是件好事情呢！"

一年以后，很多年轻人都被征兵入伍，多数人都死在战场上。塞翁的儿子却因为残疾免除兵役，从而保全了性命。

 A Foolish Man Buys Shoes

郑人买履

〖A Foolish Man Buys Shoes〗

In the past there lived a foolish man in a small kingdom called Zheng. One day he wanted to buy himself a pair of new shoes. He measured his feet with a ruler first and wrote down his size. But he was in such a hurry to set out that he left it at home.

zhèng rén mǎi lǚ
郑 人 买 履

guò qù   yǒu yí gè xiǎo guó jiào zhèng guó   nà lǐ zhù zhe yí gè yú hàn   yì tiān   tā xiǎng qù mǎi yī
过去，有一个小国叫郑国，那里住着一个愚汉。一天，他想去买一

shuāng xīn xié   biàn xiān yòng chǐ zi liáng yí xià zì jǐ de jiǎo   rán hòu huà le yí gè dǐ yàng   jì xià chǐ
双 新鞋，便先用尺子量一下自己的脚，然后画了一个底样，记下尺

mǎ   yóu yú tā zǒu dé tài jí   jìng jiāng chǐ mǎ là zài jiā lǐ
码。由于他走得太急，竟将尺码落在家里。

When he arrived at a shoe shop, he felt in his pocket only to find that it was not there. So he said apologetically, "I have left the measurement at home and don't know the size. I'll fetch it in one minute." With these words he hurried off as fast as his legs could carry him.

dào le xié diàn tā yì tāo dōu fā xiàn chǐ mǎ là zài jiā lǐ le tā bàoqiàn de shuō wǒ jiāng chǐ
到了鞋店，他一掏兜，发现尺码落在家里了。他抱歉地说，"我将尺

mǎ là zài jiā lǐ le wǒ bù zhī dào xié de chǐ cùn wǒ mǎshàng jiù qù qǔ shuōzhe biàn fēi yě shì de wǎng
码落在家里了，我不知道鞋的尺寸。我马上就去取。"说着便飞也似地往

huí gǎn
回赶。

He ran back home, found it, and then ran to the shop again. But still it took him quite a while and by then the shop was already closed. He had gone to all this trouble for nothing and did not get his shoes.

Then someone asked him, "Did you buy the shoes for yourself or someone else?" "For myself, of course." he answered. "Then why didn't you just try on the shoes yourself?"

他赶到家，找到底样，又费段时间返回鞋店。等到他赶回鞋店时，鞋店已关门了，鞋也就没有买成。

于是有人问他："你是给自己买鞋还是给别人买鞋呢？""当然是给自己买喽！"愚汉回答说。"那你用自己的脚去试鞋子不就行了吗？"

10

The Frog in the Shallow Well
井底之蛙

〖The Frog in the Shallow Well〗

A frog who lived in a shallow well met a turtle who lived in the sea. The Frog said, "I am so happy! When I am happy, I jump about on the railing beside the well. When I am tired, I rest in the holes on the broken wall of the well. If I jump into the water, it comes up to my armpits and holds up my cheeks. If I walk in the mud, it covers up my feet. I look around at the wriggly worms, crabs and tadpoles, etc, and none of them can com-

jǐng dǐ zhī wā
井底之蛙

一只青蛙住在井里。有一天,青蛙在井边遇上了一只从海里来的大龟。

青蛙说:"我住在这里多么快乐啊!高兴的时候,可以在井栏边跳跃玩耍;疲倦的时候,就回到井里睡在砖洞里。如果我跳入水中,水流穿过我的腋窝,支撑我的头部。如果我在泥地上走,泥浆便盖过我的脚面。我看看

pare with me. Moreover, I am lord of this trough of water and I stand tall in this shallow well. My happiness is full. My dear turtle, why don't you come often and take a look around my place?"

Before the turtle from the sea could get its left foot in the well, its right knee got stuck. It hesitated and retreated. The turtle told the frog:

zhōuwéi de qiūyǐn lā   pángxiè lā   háiyǒu kē dǒuděng   tā men nǎ li nénggēn wǒ bǐ ne   wǒ shì zhè ge jǐng lǐ
周围的蚯蚓啦 、螃蟹啦 、还有蝌蚪 等 , 他们哪里 能 跟我比呢 ？ 我是这个井里

de zhǔrén   zì yóu zì zài de hǎo bù xiāoyáokuài lè   qīn ài de hǎi guī   nǐ chángdào wǒ de jǐng lǐ lái yóuwán
的主人 , 自由自在的好不逍遥快乐！ 亲爱的海龟 , 你 常 到我的井里来游玩

ba
吧 ！ ”

dà guī shì zhe bǎ tā de zuǒ jiǎoshēn jìn jǐng lǐ qù   dàn shì yòu tuǐ bèi bànzhù le   tā chí chúzhe tuì què xià
大龟试着把它的左脚 伸进井里去 , 但是右腿被绊住了 。它踟蹰着退却下

lái   duì qīng wā shuō
来 , 对青蛙说 ：

"Have you seen the sea before? Even a distance of a thousand li cannot give you an idea of the sea's width; even a height of a thousand zhang cannot give you an idea of its depth. In the time of the Xia dynasty, there were floods nine years out of ten, but the waters in the sea did not increase much. In the time of the Shang dynasty there were droughts seven years out of eight, but the waters in the sea did not decrease much. The real happiness is to live in the sea."

Hearing these words, the frog of the shallow well was shocked into realizing his own insignificance and ignorance.

nǐ jiànguò dà hǎi ma   hǎi de guǎng dà   hé zhǐ qiān lǐ   hǎi de shēn dù   hé zhǐ qiānzhàng   xià cháo
“你见过大海吗？海的广大，何止千里；海的深度，何止千丈。夏朝

shí hòu   měi shí niánzhōngyǒu jiǔ nián fā dà shuǐ   dànshì hǎi lǐ de shuǐ bìng bù zhǎng   dào hòu lái shāngcháo   měi
时候，每十年中有九年发大水，但是海里的水并不涨；到后来商朝，每

bā niánzhōngyǒu qī nián dà hàn   hǎi lǐ de shuǐ   yě méiyǒushǎo le duōshǎo   zhùzài dà hǎi lǐ   cái shì zhēnzhèng
八年中有七年大旱，海里的水，也没有少了多少。住在大海里，才是真正

de kuài lè ne
的快乐呢！”

qīng wā tīng le hǎi guī de huà   chī jīng bù xiǎo   kāi shǐ rèn shi dào zì jǐ de qiǎn bó hé wú zhī
青蛙听了海龟的话，吃惊不小，开始认识到自己的浅薄和无知。

14

Aping a Beauty

东施效颦

〖Aping a Beauty〗

Xi Shi, a famous beauty, had a pain in her bosom, so she had a frown on her face putting her hands on her bosom when she went out.

An ugly girl named Dong Shi lived nearby. She saw Xi Shi and thought she looked very beautiful. Therefore when she went home, she also put her hands on her bosom and made a frown on her face. People in the neighborhood saw her ugly gesture and stayed away from her.

Dong Shi only knew Xi Shi's frown looked beautiful but she did not know the reason for her beauty.

dōng shī xiào pín

东 施 效 颦

古代有名的美女西施有一次犯了心口疼的毛病。出门的时候，她用手捂住胸口，双眉紧锁。

住在附近的丑女东施看见了，很羡慕她的美丽，于是也学着西施的姿势，皱眉捂胸走回家。邻居们看到东施扭捏难看的样子，都远远地躲开她。

东施只知道西施皱眉看起来很美，她没有弄明白，西施究竟美在哪里。

 His Spear Against His Shield
自相矛盾

〖His Spear Against His Shield〗

A man from the state of Chu had a spear and a shield for sale in the market. He was loud in praise of his shield. "My shield is so strong that nothing can pierce it through." He also sang praises of his spear: "My spear is so strong that it can pierce through anything."

"What would happen," he was then asked by another man, "if we use your spear to pierce your shield?"

It was impossible for the man from Chu to answer this question.

zì xiāngmáodùn
自相矛盾

有个楚国人拿了一支长矛和一个盾牌，在集市上出售。他举起盾牌，大声叫卖："我的盾牌最坚固不过了。无论多么锋利的武器也刺不透我的盾牌！"他又举起长矛大声夸耀："我的长矛最锋利不过了。无论多么坚固的盾牌，我的长矛也能刺透它！"

这时有人问他："如果用您的长矛来刺您的盾牌，会是怎样的结果呢？"

楚国人顿时回答不上来了。

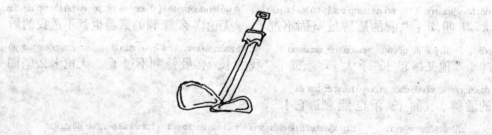

Making His Mark
刻舟求剑

〖Making His Mark〗

A man from the state of Chu was crossing a river. In the boat, his sword fell into the water. Immediately he made a mark on the boat. He said, "This is where my sword fell off!"

After the boat stopped moving, he jumped into the water to look for his sword at the place where he had marked the boat and undoubtedly he couldn't find it.

In his eyes, the boat had moved but the sword kept staying at the place where he had marked! How foolish it is to look for a sword in this way!

kè zhōu qiú jiàn
刻舟求剑

一个楚国人，乘船渡江时不小心把他的剑掉进了河里。他马上在船沿上作上一个记号，并说："这儿就是我掉剑的地方。"

船停后，这个楚人跳下水去，在船沿上作记号的位置寻找他的剑，无疑他怎么也不会找到他的剑了。

在他看来，船开走了，而他那柄剑一直保持在刻记号的地方。用这种方法来找剑，难道不是很愚蠢吗？

中国传统文化经典故事100篇·英汉对照

Ostrich Logic
掩耳盗铃

〖Ostrich Logic〗

At the time the Spring and Autumn Period when Fan, a nobleman of the state of Jin, became a fugitive, a thief stole into his house and only found a bell. He wanted to carry it off on his back. But the bell was too big for him to be moved.

When he tried to knock it into pieces with a hammer there was a loud clanging sound. He was afraid that someone would hear the noise and find him, so he immediately covered his own ears. Then he was seized when people heard the noise.

To worry about other people hearing the noise is understandable, but to worry about himself hearing the noise isn't absurd?

yǎn ěr dào líng
掩耳盗铃

chūn qiū shí qī　　yǒu gè xiǎo tōu dào jìn guó luò nàn de fàn xìng guì zú jiā li tōu dōng xī　　jiē guǒ zhǐ fā xiàn yì
春 秋 时 期 , 有 个 小 偷 到 晋 国 落 难 的 范 姓 贵 族 家 里 偷 东 西 , 结 果 只 发 现 一

kǒu dà zhōng　　　tā xiǎng bǎ zhōng bān zǒu　　kě shì zhōng tài dà le　　zěn me bān yě bān bú dòng
口 大 钟 。 他 想 把 钟 搬 走 , 可 是 钟 太 大 了 , 怎 么 搬 也 搬 不 动 。

tā zhǎo lái yì bǎ dà chuí shì tú bǎ dà zhōng qiāo suì　　bú liào dà zhōng měng rán fā chū yī shēng jù xiǎng　　xiǎo
他 找 来 一 把 大 锤 试 图 把 大 钟 敲 碎 , 不 料 大 钟 猛 然 发 出 一 声 巨 响 。 小

tōu pà bié rén tīng dào zhè xiǎng shēng fā xiàn tā　　yú shì tā lì jí yòng shuāng shǒu bǎ zì yǐ de ěr duo wǔ zhù　　hǎo
偷 怕 别 人 听 到 这 响 声 发 现 他 , 于 是 他 立 即 用 双 手 把 自 己 的 耳 朵 捂 住 , 好

ràng zì jǐ tīng bú jiàn zhōng xiǎng　　jié guǒ rén men tīng dào zhōng shēng hòu　　pǎo lái bǎ tā zhuā zhù le
让 自 己 听 不 见 钟 响 。 结 果 人 们 听 到 钟 声 后 , 跑 来 把 他 抓 住 了 。

dān xīn bié rén tīng dào zhōng shēng kě yǐ lǐ jiě　　ér dān xīn zì jǐ tīng dào zhōng shēng bú shì hěn huāng miù ma
担 心 别 人 听 到 钟 声 可 以 理 解 , 而 担 心 自 己 听 到 钟 声 不 是 很 荒 谬 吗 ?

中国传统文化经典故事100篇·英汉对照

22

A Mantis Blocking a Chariot

螳臂当车

〖A Mantis Blocking a Chariot〗

This is a legendary story dating back to the Spring and Autumn Period. Once, the King of Qi went out to hunt with his men. The carriages were going along, when suddenly a mantis stood in the middle of the road with its sickle-like forelegs opened. It was obvious that it was trying to fight against the carriage to hold it back. Surprised at the case, the King of Qi ordered the carriages to stop and asked what creature it was. He was told it was called "mantis" and that it would go well up to bridle decisively when it was challenged.

táng bì dāng chē
螳臂当车

zhè gù shì fā shēng zài chūnqiū shí qī qí guó de guówáng yǒu yí cì dài rén chū qù dǎ liè tú zhōng hū rán
这故事发生在春秋时期，齐国的国王有一次带人出去打猎。途中，忽然

lù páng tiào chū lái yì zhī xiǎo chóng zi zhāng kāi liǎng tiáo liàn dāo xíng de bì bǎng hěn xiǎn rán tā shì tú zǔ lán
路旁跳出来一只小虫子，张开两条镰刀形的臂膀。很显然，它试图阻拦

qián jìn zhōng de chē lún zi qí wáng kàn jiàn le gǎn dào hěn qí guài jiù mìng lìng jiāng chē zi tíng xià lái qí
前进中的车轮子。齐王看见了感到很奇怪，就命令将车子停下来。齐

wáng wèn dào zhè shì yì zhī shén me chóng zi rén men gào sù tā nà shì yì zhī táng láng tā kàn jiàn chē zi
王问道："这是一只什么虫子？"人们告诉他那是一只螳螂。它看见车子

lái le bù zhī dào gǎn kuài duǒ bì hái shàng lái zǔ dǎng zhēn shì bú yào mìng lq
来了，不知道赶快躲避，还上来阻挡，真是不要命啦！

The King sighed with exclamation at its braveness. He mused a moment and added: "It's a great pity that it is not more than an insect. If it were a man, he must be the bravest warrior in the world!" Then the King ordered his carriages to drive around it to leave the mantis there standing martially.

齐王感慨螳螂的勇敢精神，沉思了片刻，叹道："很遗憾，它不过是一只昆虫，如果这是一个人，那一定是世上最勇敢的士兵！"他命令车夫绕开螳螂，留下勇敢的螳螂独自站在路中。

As time passed, the meaning of the phrase "A Mantis Blocking a Chariot" changed to mean its opposite. Now it doesn't refer to the spirit of braveness but mocks that someone overrates himself and tries to hold back an overwhelmingly superior force.

后来人们在提到"螳臂当车"这个成语时，往往是反其意而用之。人们用这个成语不是指勇敢精神而是讽刺那些自不量力、企图阻止无法抗拒的力量的人。

 A Fond Dream of Nanke
南柯一梦

〖A Fond Dream of Nanke〗

In the Tang Dynasty, there lived a person called Chun Yufen. One day, his friends came to celebrate his birthday, and Chun Yufen was drinking under an old pagoda tree. When he became drunk, he fell asleep. Dazzledly, Chun Yufen met with two atomies who took him into the giant hole in the tree, to have a ride to the great Kingdom of Pagoda. Chun Yufen found himself in a fairy world with many red gates, magnificent palaces, luxuriant pavilions, and beautiful gardens.

nán kē yí mèng
南柯一梦

在中国唐朝，有个人叫淳于梦。一天他过生日，在大槐树下摆下宴席，和朋友饮酒作乐，好不快活。喝醉了之后，他便睡着了。迷迷糊糊之中，他突然感觉有两个使者请他上车，马车朝大槐树下一个树洞驶去，驶向"槐安国"。他发现树洞里另有一番仙境：有许多朱红色的大门，大门里面是华丽的宫殿，周围是亭台楼阁和美丽的花园。

The king appreciated him so much that he was named the mayor of Nanke, a small town in the Kingdom. Soon after, he married the king's beautiful daughter. Chun Yufen was so happy with the life there that he totally forgot his hometown. Twenty years passed, and Chun Yufen stayed as the very successful mayor of Nanke, making everything there in perfect order, and raised a big family of 5 sons and 2 daughters.

However, the kingdom was invaded by another one and Chun Yufen had to lead the troops to hold out the enemies. Unfortunately, his troops were defeated and at the same time his wife died. Chun Yufen decided to leave the Kingdom of Pagoda. He was sent home by the 2 atomies.

国王非常欣赏淳于棼，封他为"南柯郡太守"，国家里的一个小城。后来，国王还将美丽的公主许配给他。淳于棼与公主过得非常幸福以致完全忘了自己的家乡。淳于棼上任南柯郡太守后，前后二十年的时间，把南柯郡治理得井井有条，还和公主生了五个儿子，两个女儿。

不料，有个国家突然入侵，淳于棼不得不率兵迎击，不过他还是打了败仗。这时公主又不幸去世了。淳于棼决定离开"槐安国"，仍是由两名使者送行。

As soon as he arrived home, he suddenly woke up to realize what had happened was just a dream. It was only a short nap, even though in his dream he had experienced a whole 20 years of life. Chun Yufen's friends were interested to hear his dream. They looked down the tree, found an ant nest, connected to a smaller nest in the south direction. Obviously, these nests explained what "Pagoda Kingdom" and "Nanke" really were!

chún yú fén huí dào jiā zhōng   tū rán jīng xǐng guò lái   yuán lái shì yī chǎng mèng   bù guò shì xiǎo shuì yì huì er
淳于棼回到家中，突然惊醒过来，原来是一场梦。不过是小睡一会儿，

ér mèng zhōng jīng lì què zhěng zhěng èr shí nián   chún yú fén bǎ mèng jìng gào sù péng yǒu   dà jiā gǎn dào shí fēn yǒu qù   yì
而梦中经历却整整二十年。淳于棼把梦境告诉朋友，大家感到十分有趣，一

qí zhǎo dào dà huái shù xià   wā chū yī gè hěn dà de mǎ yǐ dòng   páng biān yǒu kǒng   tōng xiàng nán bian   nà li yǒu yī gè
齐找到大槐树下，挖出一个很大的蚂蚁洞，旁边有孔，通向南边，那里有一个

xiǎo mǎ yǐ dòng   hěn xiǎn rán   zhè jiù shì suǒ wèi de   huái ān guó   nán kē jùn
小蚂蚁洞。很显然，这就是所谓的"槐安国"和"南柯郡"！

 Fish for the Moon in the Well
水中捞月

〖Fish for the Moon in the Well〗

One evening, the clever man, Afanti went to fetch some water from the well. When he looked into the well, he saw the moon sunk in the well, round and shiny. He was so shocked that he quickly went home to get a rope, then lowered it into the well to fish for the moon. After some time of hunting for the moon, Afanti felt that something was caught by the bucket. He was excited and pulled hard by the rope. Due to the excessive pulling, the rope broke apart and Afanti fell flat on his back. From that position, Afanti saw the moon again high in the sky.

He proudly said, "It finally came back to its place! What a good job I did!"

shuǐ zhōng lāo yuè
水 中 捞 月

一天晚上，聪明的阿凡提提着桶去井边打水，到了井边一看，井底有一轮又亮又圆的明月。他大吃一惊，赶紧回家取了一根绳索，把桶放下井里去捞月亮。捞了一会儿，阿凡提感觉好像有东西，他很兴奋，就使劲儿地拉绳子。由于太用力绳索断了，阿凡提摔了一个跟头。他仰面朝天倒在地上，一看，月亮高高悬挂在天空中。

阿凡提得意地说道："我总算把月亮捞出来挂在天上了。"

Of ... when he has ... could point water into the well. When ... looked in the well, he saw the moon ... in the well ... and since the ... pulled it up, came to conclude to scoop ... water. So yelled while he went. I told my ... the ... After ...

A Walk Learner in Handan
邯郸学步

〚A Walk Learner in Handan〛

This story happened in the Warring States period. A young man in Shouling, a town in the state of Yan, lacked confidence in his walking style.

One day he heard that people in Handan, the capital of the state of Zhao, had an elegant way of walking. So, he went a long way there to learn.

hándānxué bù
邯郸学步

gù shì fā shēng zài zhànguóshí qī   yānguóshòulíngyǒu yí wèiniánqīngrén duì zì   jǐ zǒu lù de zī shì bù mǎn
故事发生在战国时期，燕国寿陵有一位年轻人对自己走路的姿势不满

yì   quēshǎo zì xìn xīn
意，缺少自信心。

yì tiān   tā tīngshuōzài zhàoguó de shǒu dū hándān   rénmenzǒu lù de zī shì fēi chángyōuyǎ   yú shì tā
一天，他听说在赵国的首都邯郸，人们走路的姿势非常优雅。于是，他

cháng tú bá shèdào le hándān   qù xué xí zǒu lù
长途跋涉到了邯郸，去学习走路。

Arriving in the town of Handan, he was amazed to see so many great ways of walking. The young boys walked with energy; the elderly walked with solid steps; and the women walked, rocking their hips. He was well indulged in the study all day long, following different people and learning all kinds of elegant walking styles.

yí dào hándān   tā gǎndào xīnxiān jí le   rénmen zǒu lù de zī shì gè bù xiāngtóng   lìng rén yǎn huā liáo
一到邯郸， 他感到新鲜极了， 人们走路的姿势各不相同， 令人眼花缭

luàn   xiǎohuǒ er zǒu lù bù fá jiǎojiàn   lǎorén zǒu lù bù lǚ jiāndìng   fù nǚ zǒu lù ē nuóduō zī   tā zhěng
乱。 小伙儿走路步伐矫健，老人走路步履坚定，妇女走路婀娜多姿。 他整

tiān gēn zài gè zhǒng rén hòumian   zuì xīn yú xué xí gè zhǒng yōu yǎ de zǒu lù zī tài
天跟在各种人后面，醉心于学习各种优雅的走路姿态。

Half a month passed by, and the young man suddenly felt that he hadn't learned anything. Even worse, he found himself unable to walk in his own way. So he had no choice but to crawl home.

就这样，半个月过去了，这个年轻人突然感到自己什么都没学会。更糟糕的是他发现他将自己原来走路的姿势都忘了，连走也不会走了。最终，他只好爬着回到寿陵。

 Bring the Dragons to Life by Putting Pupils in Their Eyes
画龙点睛

36

〖Bring the Dragons to Life by Putting Pupils in Their Eyes〗

During the Northern and Southern Dynasties, there was a famous painter named Zhang Sengyao. He was highly praised for his fine art by Emperor Liang Wu. The emperor often asked him to paint on the Buddhist temple walls.

One year, Zhang Sengyao was asked to paint for the temple of Andong in JinLing. He agreed and painted four dragons on the wall. Everybody appreciated the vivid dragons on the wall. However, they soon found that all these four dragons didn't have pupils in

huà lóng diǎn jīng
画龙点睛

zài nán běi cháo shí qī　 liáng cháo yǒu yí wèi zhùmíng de dà huà jiā míng jiào zhāng sēng yáo　 dāng shí de huáng
在南北朝时期， 梁 朝有一位著名的大画家名叫 张 僧繇。当时的皇

dì liáng wǔ dì hěn xīn shǎng tā de huì huà yì shù　 jīng cháng ràng tā wèi sì miào huà bì huà
帝 梁 武帝很欣 赏 他的绘画艺术，经 常 让他为寺庙 画壁画。

yǒu yì nián　 liáng wǔ dì yào zhāng sēng yáo wéi jīn líng de ān dōng sì zuò huà　 tā dā ying xià lái　 zài sì miào
有一年 ， 梁 武帝要 张 僧繇为金陵的安东寺做画 。 他答应下来，在寺庙

de qiáng bì shàng huà le sì tiáo lóng　 rén men dōu chēng zàn zhāng sēng yáo zhè sì tiáo lóng huà de xǔ xǔ rú shēng　 kě
的 墙 壁 上 画了四条龙 。人们都 称 赞 张 僧繇这四条龙画得栩栩如生 。可

shì　 dà jiā hěn kuài jiù fā xiàn zhè sì tiáo lóng quán dōu méi yǒu yǎn jīng　 biàn fēn fēn wèn tā
是 ， 大 家 很 快 就 发 现 这 四 条 龙 全 都 没 有 眼 睛 ， 便 纷 纷 问 他，

37

their eyes. They asked Zhang, and he replied, "Well, they will fly away if the pupils are put in." Nobody believed him. At the people's request, Zhang Sengyao had to take up his paintbrush to begin dotting pupils onto the dragons' eyes. After he was finished with the second dragon, a loud thunderbolt struck the temple. The two dragons with pupils precipitated into a cloud of rolls of thunder and lightning before Zhang could drop the paintbrush. The crowd was disordered into a mess.

张僧繇解释说："给龙点上眼睛，这些龙会飞走的。"大家听后都不相信，坚持要他给龙的眼睛点上。张僧繇无奈，只好提起画笔，开始给两条龙点眼睛。他刚点过第二条龙的眼睛，突然间雷鸣电闪。张僧繇还未来得及放下画笔，两条带眼睛的龙便跳出来和雷电声相应和，人们惊恐万状，乱作一团。

中国传统文化经典故事100篇·英汉对照

A loud crash was heard and the wall toppled into pieces in the middle. The dragons writhed for a while and flew away high in the sky. People couldn't believe what they just saw. They looked onto the wall, and fortunately, the two dragons without pupils still remained there peacefully.

yì shēng jù xiǎng zhī hòu   sì miào de qiáng bì cóng zhōng jiān liè kāi   liǎng tiáo lóng zhāng yá wǔ zhǎo de fēi
一 声 巨 响 之 后 , 寺 庙 的 墙 壁 从 中 间 裂 开 ， 两 条 龙 张 牙 舞 爪 地 飞

xiàng tiān kōng   rén men jiǎn zhí wú fǎ xiāng xìn zì jǐ de yǎn jīng   zài kàn kan qiáng shàng   zhǐ shèng xià   méi yǒu
向 天 空 。 人 们 简 直 无 法 相 信 自 己 的 眼 睛 。 再 看 看 墙 上 ， 只 剩 下 没 有

bèi diǎn shàng yǎn jīng de liǎng tiáo lóng le
被 点 上 眼 睛 的 两 条 龙 了 。

A Wily Hare Has Three Burrows

狡兔三窟

〚A Wily Hare Has Three Burrows〛

This story happened in the Warring States Period. Meng Changjun, the Prime Minister of the Qi State, one day sent his man Feng Huan to collect land tax from tenant farmers of his home town.

When Feng Huan got to the farm, he collected the farmers and declared: "All the tenancy contracts are to be demolished at once!" Cheers burst out among the astonished and happy farmers since they owed too much to their government.

jiǎo tù sān kū
狡兔三窟

gù shì fā shēng zài zhànguóshí qī   yī tiān   qí guó de xiàngguómèngchángjūnpàimén kè fénghuān qù tā de
故事发生在战国时期。一天,齐国的相国孟尝君派门客冯欢去他的

lǎo jiā xiàngdiàn hù shōu zū
老家向佃户收租。

fénghuāndào le mèngchángjūn de lǎo jiā   bǎ diàn hù zhào jí qǐ lái duì tā menxuān bù   bǎ suǒyǒu de
冯欢到了孟尝君的老家,把佃户召集起来对他们宣布:"把所有的

diàn zū qì yuēdōu ná chū lái   tǒngtǒngshāohuǐ   zhài hù menyòujīngyòu xǐ   yīn wéi tā menqiàn le guān fǔ tài
佃租契约都拿出来,统统烧毁。"债户们又惊又喜,因为他们欠了官府太

duō de zhài
多的债。

When Feng Huan returned and told the host about what he had done, Prime Minister Meng Changjun was angry about it. "Why did you do that?" the minister asked. "Well, I did not bring you any fortune by doing that." Feng Huan responded, "But I really won the loyalty of your farmers, which is more valuable than the tax money."

féng huān huí qù yǐ hòu xiàng mèng cháng jūn bào gào le shì qíng de jīng guò   mèng cháng jūn shí fēn nǎo huǒ   wèn
冯 欢 回 去 以 后 向 孟 尝 君 报 告 了 事 情 的 经 过 , 孟 尝 君 十 分 恼 火 , 问

dào   nǐ wèi shén me yào zhè yàng zuò   féng huān huí dá shuō   wǒ suī rán méi néng gěi nín dài lái cái fù
道 : "你 为 什 么 要 这 样 做 ? " 冯 欢 回 答 说 : "我 虽 然 没 能 给 您 带 来 财 富 ,

què zhēn zhèng yíng dé le mín xīn   duì nín ér yán   mín xīn bú shì bǐ zū jīn gèng yǒu jià zhí ma
却 真 正 赢 得 了 民 心 , 对 您 而 言 , 民 心 不 是 比 租 金 更 有 价 值 吗 ? "

Meng Changjun was dismissed from office the next year, so he decided to go back to his hometown. When he arrived at his demesne, he was surprised to see the farmers were on both sides of the road welcoming him warmly. At the sight, Meng Changjun felt greatly moved, and he asked Feng Huan for the reason. "This is the reward for your charities." This reminded Meng Changjun of what he had forgotten the year before. He could not help giving Fenghuan the thumbs up.

dì èr nián mèng cháng jūn shī chǒng bèi qí wáng miǎn qù le xiàng guó zhí wù mèng cháng jūn jué dìng huí
第二年，孟尝君失宠，被齐王免去了相国职务。孟尝君决定回

dào zì jǐ de fēng dì fù xián hái méi jìn chéng lǎo yuǎn jiù kàn jiàn rén fú lǎo xié yòu jiā dào huān yíng tā cǐ
到自己的封地赋闲。还没进城，老远就看见人扶老携幼，夹道欢迎他。此

qíng cǐ jǐng lìng mèng cháng jūn shí fēn gǎn dòng tā wèn féng huān yīn hé shòu dào bǎi xìng rú cǐ ài dài féng huān
情此景令孟尝君十分感动，他问冯欢因何受到百姓如此爱戴。冯欢

shuō zhè shì nín yì jǔ de huí bào mèng cháng jūn yǐ jiāng qù nián de shì qíng wàng diào bù yóu de shù qǐ
说："这是您义举的回报。"孟尝君已将去年的事情忘掉，不由得竖起

dà mu zhǐ chēng zàn féng huān de jiàn shi
大拇指称赞冯欢的见识。

At this time Feng Huan continued, "A wily hare which has three burrows can keep itself safe. But now you have only one. So you must struggle to get the other two, one in the state of Qin, and the other in the state of Qi."

Feng Huan paid a visit to the State of Qin, said to the king, "Meng Changjun was the main reason for Qi's prosperity in recent years. Now that he is treated badly by the king of Qi, you should acquire him before it's too late!" The king of Qin agreed with him and sent people to hire Meng Changjun.

这时，冯欢又说："狡兔筑三窟，才有安全。而您现在只有一窟，您必须尽快建造另外的两个，一个是秦，一个是齐。"

随后冯欢就到秦国去见了秦王。他对秦王说道："齐国近年来治理得这么昌盛，全是孟尝君的功劳。既然齐王这么对待他，您就该乘机趁早收留他。秦王同意冯欢的观点，立刻派遣使者前去聘请孟尝君。

Then Feng Huan immediately went to the king of Qi and said to him, "Don't you feel worried? Your former Prime Minister, who has all the confidential information about our state, is about to take a position in the hostile Qin State!" The king of Qi acted quickly to reappoint Meng Changjun as the prime minister of the state. Afterwards, Feng Huan said to Meng Changjun, his master, "Now, all the three burrows have been built, and you should be safe now!" It was said that Meng Changjun held the post for the rest of his life and his tenants lived in peace.

之后，冯欢立刻赶到齐国求见齐王。他对齐王说道："您不觉得担心吗？咱们前任相国孟尝君对国家机密了如指掌，真要当了秦国相国的话，咱们齐国不就完了吗？"齐王连忙派人把孟尝君接回来，重新拜他为相国。然后，冯欢对孟尝君说："现在，三窟都已建成，您应该有安全感啦！"据说孟尝君在后来的岁月中一直稳坐其位，他的门客们也都过得很太平。

 The Gentleman on the Beam
梁上君子

〖The Gentleman on the Beam〗

In the Eastern Han Dynasty, there lived a man named Chen Shi, who was respected by people for his fine morality and good reputation. After his retirement, he lived in his hometown. One year, turmoil and war took place because of a famine. Robberies and thieves were rampant in that area.

liáng shàng jūn zǐ
梁上君子

dōng hàn shí qī   yǒu yí gè jiào zuò chén shí de rén   tā dé gāo wàng zhòng   hěn shòu rén men de jìng
东汉时期，有一个叫做陈寔的人。他德高望重，很受人们的敬

zhòng   tuì xiū yǐ hòu   tā fù xián zài jiā   yǒu yì nián chén shí de jiā xiāng nào jī huang   zhàn zhēng   sāo luàn
重。退休以后，他赋闲在家。有一年陈寔的家乡闹饥荒，战争、骚乱

hùn chéng yì tuán   yì shí jiān tōu dào sì qǐ
混成一团，一时间偷盗四起。

47

One night a thief entered the house of Chen Shi through a window.   The thief was about to start his deal when Chen Shi got up to relieve himself.   The thief hid himself on the beam.   Chen Shi noticed the thief but pretended not to.   After he tied the belt around his waist,   instead of calling the thief down,   he called his sons up and then spoke out to them, "Listen!" the father declared. "As a man, one should act straightly and firmly. He should do good deeds all his life." The address made by the father in the middle of the night puzzled the sons. The father raised his voice and continued, "You must remember that one can be short of property, however, he must stand on his dignity."

一天晚上，有一个小偷从窗户溜进陈寔的家。小偷刚要动手，这时陈寔起来解手，小偷便躲在屋梁上面。陈寔发现屋梁上面有人，却假装没有看到。陈寔系上腰带后，没有惊动小偷，反而把儿子们都叫醒，对他们说："你们听着，做人要走得正，行得正。一个人要一生一世做好事不做坏事。"儿子们面面相觑，对父亲半夜三更把他们唤醒说这些话很是不解。陈寔提高声音继续说："记住了！一个人可以贫穷，但是尊严不能丢！"

The thief felt very sorry and ashamed of what he did.   He began to weep on the beam. Later, he climbed down and knelt before Chen Shi, "I'm terribly sorry, but that is all because of the famine,   I beg for your mercy." Chen Shi forgave him,   gave him some food and cloth, and let him go.

xiǎotōu duì zì jǐ de suǒzuòsuǒwéi gǎndào qiàn jiù hé xiū kuì   tā kāi shǐ zài liángshàng kū qì   hòu lái
小偷对自己的所作所为感到歉疚和羞愧。 他开始在 梁 上 哭泣。后来，

tā cóng wū liángshàng pá xià lái   guì zài chén shí de qiánmian   chén lǎo ye   duì bù qǐ   wǒ shì yīn wéi bèi
他从屋梁 上 爬下来，跪在陈寔的前面："陈老爷，对不起！我是因为被

shēnghuó bī de méi fǎ zi   qǐng nín yuánliàng wǒ   chén shí bú dàn méiyǒu zé mà xiǎotōu   hái gěi le tā yì xiē
生活逼的没法子，请您原谅我！" 陈 寔不但没有责骂小偷，还给了他一些

yī shí ràng tā qù le
衣食让他去了。

The crickets were smaller and... He... were on the
branch. Later, he climbed down and went over... Then Sir... "I hate... story because it is
all because of the story... The... for you name... Chen Shi forgave him, gave him food
and clothes and let him go.

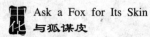 Ask a Fox for Its Skin
与狐谋皮

〖Ask a Fox for Its Skin〗

Long ago, there lived a young man called Lisheng who had a beautiful wife. One day, she had an idea that a coat of fox fur would look pretty on her, so she asked her husband to get her one. But the coat was rare and too expensive. The helpless husband was forced to walk around on the hillside. Just at the moment, a fox was walking by. He affectionately said to the fox: "Well, dear fox, let's make an agreement. Could you offer me a sheet of your skin?" But the moment he finished his words, the fox ran away as quickly as it could into the forest.

与狐谋皮

古时候有一个叫李生的人，娶了一位漂亮的妻子。一天，妻子突发奇想，认为她穿上狐皮大衣一定很好看，就请求丈夫给她买一件。狐皮不仅稀少而且价格昂贵。丈夫非常无助地在山脚下转悠，恰巧这时，碰到了一只狐狸，他便十分亲热地对它说："亲爱的狐狸，咱们商量一下，你可不可以送我一张狐皮？"他的话刚一说完，狐狸就飞快地逃走了，一头钻进树林里去了。

中国传统文化经典故事100篇·英汉对照

 Zhuangzhou Dreamed a Butterfly
庄周梦蝶

〖Zhuangzhou Dreamed a Butterfly〗

One day at sunset, Zhuangzhou dozed off and dreamed that he turned into a butterfly. He flapped his wings and made sure he was a butterfly. He had such a joyful feeling as he fluttered about that he completely forgot that he was Zhuangzi. Soon though, he realized that that proud butterfly was really Zhuangzi who dreamed he was a butterfly. Or was it a butterfly who dreamed he was Zhuangzi?

Maybe Zhuangzi was the butterfly? and maybe the butterfly was Zhungzi? This is what is meant by the "transformation of things."

zhuāngzhōumèng dié

庄 周 梦 蝶

一日傍晚，庄周打盹儿梦见自己变成一只蝴蝶。他扑打扑打翅膀，确信自己已经变成一只蝴蝶。这时他十分惬意，飘飘然竟完全忘记了自己是庄子。一会儿醒来，他明白了，那只骄傲的蝴蝶正是梦见自己变成蝴蝶的庄子。或许是蝴蝶做梦自己变成了庄子也未可知。

庄周是蝴蝶？亦或蝴蝶是庄周？这正是所谓的"事物转换"的道理啊！

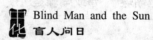

中国传统文化经典故事100篇·英汉对照

Blind Man and the Sun
盲人问日

〖Blind Man and the Sun〗

Once upon a time, there was a blind man who did not know what the Sun is, so he asked other people to explain.

máng rén wèn rì
盲人问日

很久以前，有一个生来就失明的盲人，从来没有见过太阳。他问别人："太阳是什么样子的？"

One man said, "The Sun is shaped like a copper plate." So the blind man banged on a copper plate, and listened to its clanging sound. Later when he heard the sound of a temple bell, he thought that must be the Sun. Another man said, "The Sun gives out light just like a candle." So the blind man held a candle to feel its shape. Later when he picked up a flute, he thought that this must be the Sun.

nà rén gào su tā　　tài yang de xíng zhuàng xiàng tóng pán　　tā qiāo qiāo tóng pán　　tīng jiàn le tóng pán dīng
那人告诉他："太阳的形状像铜盘。"他敲敲铜盘，听见了铜盘叮

dīng dāng dāng de shēng yīn　　hòu lái　　tā tīng jiàn le miào lǐ de zhōng shēng　　jiù yǐ wéi zhè shì tài yang le　　yòu yǒu
叮当当的声音。后来，他听见了庙里的钟声，就以为这是太阳了。又有

yí gè rén gào su tā　　tài yang xiàng là zhú yí yàng fā guāng　　tā mō mō là zhú　　gǎn shòu dào le tā de xíng
一个人告诉他："太阳像蜡烛一样发光。"他摸摸蜡烛，感受到了它的形

zhuàng　　hòu lái　　tā mō dào le yì zhī duǎn dí　　jiù yǐ wéi shì tài yang le
状。后来，他摸到了一支短笛，就以为是太阳了。

Yet we know that the Sun is vastly different from a bell or a flute; but a blind man does not understand the difference because he has never seen the Sun and only has heard it described.

kě shì wǒ men zhī dao tài yang yǔ zhōng shēng huò dí zi shì duō me de bù tóng a dàn shì máng rén cóng lái méi yǒu
可是我们知道太阳与钟声或笛子是多么的不同啊！但是盲人从来没有

jiàn guo tài yang zhǐ shì tīng bié rén miáo shù ér yǐ suǒ yǐ cái zào chéng zhè yàng de wù jiě
见过太阳，只是听别人描述而已，所以才造成这样的误解。

中国传统文化经典故事100篇·英汉对照

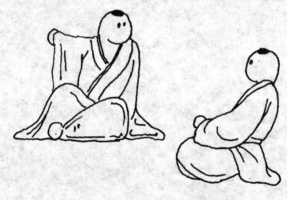

An Argument about the Sun
二童辩日

〖An Argument about the Sun〗

When Confucius was traveling in the eastern part of the country,　he came upon two children in a heated argument, so he asked them to tell him what it was about.

"I think," said one child, "that the sun is near to us at daybreak and far away from us at noon."

二童辩日

èr tóngbiàn rì

孔子东游的途中，见到两个小孩儿在面红耳赤地争论什么，就走上前去，问他们在争论什么。

"我认为太阳在黎明的时候离我们最近，而在正午时离我们最远。"一个小孩儿说。

The other contended that the sun was far away at dawn and nearby at midday.

"When the sun first appears," said one child, "it is as big as the canopy of a carriage, but at noon it is only the size of a plate or a bowl. Well, isn't it true that objects far away seem smaller while those nearby seem bigger?"

lìng yí gè xiǎohái er lì jí zhēngbiànshuō wǒ rènwéi tài yang zài lí míng de shíhou lí wǒmen zuì yuǎn
另一个小孩儿立即争辩说:"我认为太阳在黎明的时候离我们最远,

ér zài zhèngwǔ shí lí wǒmen zuì jìn
而在正午时离我们最近。"

yí gè xiǎohái er shuō tài yang gāng chū lái shí xiàng ge dà yuán chēpéng děng dào zhèngwǔ shí xiàng ge
一个小孩儿说:"太阳刚出来时像个大圆车篷,等到正午时像个

pán zi huò yú zhè bú shì yuǎnchù de xiǎo ér jìnchù de dà de dào lǐ ma
盘子或盂,这不是远处的小而近处的大的道理吗?"

"When the sun comes out," pointed out the other, "it is very cool, but at midday it is as hot as putting your hand in boiling water. Well, isn't it true that what is nearer to us is hotter and what is farther off is cooler?"

Confucius was unable to settle the matter for them. The two children laughed at him, "Who says you are a learned man?"

lìng yí gè xiǎohái er shuō　tài yang gāng chū lái shí qīng liáng hán lěng　děng dào le zhèng wǔ　tā rè de
另 一 个 小孩儿 说 ："太 阳 刚 出 来 时 清 凉 寒 冷 ， 等 到 了 正 午 ， 它 热 得

xiàng bǎ shǒu shēn xiàng rè shuǐ lǐ yí yàng　zhè bú zhèng shì jù lí jìn de jiù jué de rè　jù lí yuǎn de jiù jué de
像 把 手 伸 向 热 水 里 一 样 。 这 不 正 是 距 离 近 的 就 觉 得 热 ， 距 离 远 的 就 觉 得

liáng de dào lǐ ma
凉 的 道理吗 ？ "

kǒng zǐ bù nénggòu duàn dìng shuí shì shuí fēi　liǎng gè xiǎohái er xiào zhe shuō　shuí shuō nǐ shì bó xué duō
孔 子 不 能 够 断 定 谁 是 谁 非 。 两 个 小孩儿 笑 着 说 ："谁 说 你 是 博 学 多

cái de rén ne
才 的 人 呢 ？ "

61

中国传统文化经典故事100篇·英汉对照

Plucking Up a Crop to Help It Grow
揠苗助长

〖Plucking Up a Crop to Help It Grow〗

A short tempered man in the Song Dynasty was very anxious for his rice crop to grow up quickly.　He thought about this day and night.　But the crop was growing much slower than he expected.

One day,　he thought of a solution to this.　He plucked up all his crop a few inches. Even though he was very tired after doing this for a whole day,　he felt very happy since the crop 'grew' higher.

His son heard about this and went to see the crop.　Unfortunately,　the leaves of the crop began to wither.

yà miáozhùzhǎng
揠 苗 助 长

sòng cháo shí　yǒu gè nóng fū　xìng zi hěn jí　tā xī wàng tián lǐ de dào miáo néng kuài kuài zhǎng gāo
宋 朝 时，有个农夫，性子很急。他希望田里的稻苗 能 快 快 长 高。

tā bái tiān hēi yè de xiǎng ya　pàn ya　què fā jué nà xiē dào miáo zhǎng de yuǎn bù rú tā suǒ qī pàn de nà yàng
他白天黑夜地 想 呀、盼呀，却发觉那些稻苗 长 得 远不如他所期盼的那样。

yì tiān　tā zhōng yú xiǎng dào yí gè　zuì jiā fāng fǎ　jiù shì jiāng dào miáo bá gāo jǐ fēn　tā gàn
一 天，他终于想到一个"最佳方法"，就是将稻苗 拔高几分。 他干

le zhěng zhěng yì tiān　suī shuō lèi de yào sǐ　kě shì　dào miáo zhǎng gāo le　tā gǎn dào fēi cháng kāi
了整 整一天，虽说累得要死，可是，"稻苗 长 高了"，他感到非常开

xīn
心。

tā ér zi tīng shuō le　gǎn kuài pǎo dào dì lǐ qù kàn　bú xìng de shì hé miáo yǐ jīng kāi shǐ kū wěi le
他儿子听 说了，赶快跑到地里去看。不幸的是禾苗已经开始枯萎了。

63

Horse Knows the Way... It Knows

A short time ago... Duke... of horses were sent... the map to
grow in valley... the mouth... the traveling night... Still by empire's... much
the word... to expect...

... every... millions... point... to... the great... top a few... held
... even the price was... other than... to a world... we... none... man... finding... did
... have... most... public...

...them... from... about... the... horse... of... CO... Funnal... B... sense of the...
...

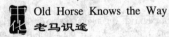
Old Horse Knows the Way
老马识途

中国传统文化经典故事100篇·英汉对照

〖Old Horse Knows the Way〗

During the Spring and Autumn Period, King Huan of Qi invaded the state of Guzhu.

The army was stuck in Guzhu for a whole year. Spring passed and winter came. When Qi's soldiers finally conquered Guzhu, they got lost and couldn't find their way back to the state of Qi.

Qi's minister Guan Zhong came up with an idea. He let the soldiers take out several old horses to lead the way. The army followed the horses closely, and finally made their way out of Guzhu, back to their homeland.

lǎo mǎ shí tú
老马识途

chūn qiū shí qī　　qí guó guó wáng qí huán gōng dài bīng gōng dǎ gū zhú guó
春秋时期，齐国国王齐桓公带兵攻打孤竹国。

qí guó dà jūn zài gū zhú guó kùn le zhěng zhěng yì nián de shí jiān　　chūn qù dōng lái　　dāng qí jūn zhōng yú dǎ
齐国大军在孤竹国困了整整一年的时间。春去冬来，当齐军终于打

bài le gū zhú guó de shí hou　　què fā xiàn tā men mí shī le fāng xiàng　　zhǎo bú dào huí qí guó de lù le
败了孤竹国的时候，却发现他们迷失了方向，找不到回齐国的路了。

zhè shí hou　　dà chén guǎn zhòng xiǎng chū le ge bàn fǎ　　tā ràng shì bīng qiān chū jǐ pǐ lǎo mǎ zài qián miàn dài
这时候，大臣管仲想出了个办法。他让士兵牵出几匹老马在前面带

lù　　dà jūn jǐn jǐn de gēn zài hòu miàn　　jiù zhè yàng zhōng yú zǒu chū le gū zhú guó　　huí dào le gù xiāng
路。大军紧紧地跟在后面，就这样终于走出了孤竹国，回到了故乡。

Playing the Lute to a Cow
对牛弹琴

〖Playing the Lute to a Cow〗

Once upon a time, there was a man who played the lute very well.

One day, he played a tune in front of a cow, hoping that the cow would appreciate it. The tune was melodious, but the cow showed no reaction, and just kept on eating grass. The man sighed, and went away.

This idiom is used to mock the idea of reasoning with stupid people or talking to the wrong audience.

duì niú tán qín
对牛弹琴

gǔ shí hòu　　yǒu yí gè rén qín tán de hěn hǎo
古时候，有一个人琴弹得很好。

yì tiān　　tā duìzheniútàn le yí duàn qǔ zi　　xī wàngniú yě néngxīnshǎng tā de jì qiǎo　　qǔ zi suī ránhěn
一天，他对着牛弹了一段曲子，希望牛也能欣赏他的技巧。曲子虽然很

hǎotīng　　dànshì niúquèháo bù lǐ huì　　zhǐ gù máitóuchī cǎo　　zhè ge rénzhǐhǎotàn le kǒu qì　lí kāi le
好听，但是牛却毫不理会，只顾埋头吃草。这个人只好叹了口气离开了。

duì niútánqín　　zhè ge chéng yǔ　　bǐ yù duì bù dǒngdào li de rénjiǎngdào li　　yě yònglái jī xiàoshuō
"对牛弹琴"这个成语，比喻对不懂道理的人讲道理，也用来讥笑说

huà de rén bú kànduì xiàng
话的人不看对象。

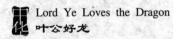
Lord Ye Loves the Dragon
叶公好龙

〖Lord Ye Loves the Dragon〗

In the Spring and Autumn Period, there lived in Chu a person named Ye Zhuliang, who addressed himself as "Lord Ye".

It is said that this Lord Ye was very fond of dragons. The walls in his house had dragons painted on them. The beams, pillars, doors, and windows were all carved with dragons. As a result, his love for dragons was spread out.

yè gōnghàolóng
叶公好龙

chūnqiūshí qī　　chǔguóyǒu ge jiào yè zhūliáng de rén　　zì chēng　　yè gōng
春秋时期，楚国有个叫叶诸梁的人，自称"叶公"。

jù shuō　　zhèwèi yè gōng ài lóngchéng pǐ　　tā jiā lǐ de qiángshànghuàzhelóng　　fáng zi de liáng
据说，这位叶公爱龙成癖。他家里的墙上画着龙，房子的梁、

zhù mén　chuāngshàngdōudiāozhelóng　　jiùzhèyàng　　yè gōng ài hàolóng de míngshēng　　bèi rénmenchuányáng
柱、门、窗上都雕着龙。就这样，叶公爱好龙的名声，被人们传扬

kāi le
开了。

When the real dragon in heaven heard of this, he was deeply moved. He decided to visit Lord Ye to thank him.

You might think that Lord Ye to be very happy to see a real dragon. However, at the very first sight of the creature, he was scared out of his wits, and ran away as fast as he could.

tiānshàng de zhēnlóng　　fīngshuōrénjiānyǒuzhème yí wèi yè gōng　　duì tā rú cǐ xǐ ài　　hěnshòugǎndòng
天 上 的 真 龙 , 听 说 人 间 有 这 么 一 位 叶 公 , 对 它 如 此 喜 爱 , 很 受 感 动 ,

jué dìng qù yè gōng jiā　　duì tā biǎoshì xiè yì
决 定 去 叶 公 家 , 对 他 表 示 谢 意 。

rénmen yě xǔ huìxiǎng yè gōngkànjiànzhēnlóngshí yí dìnghuìhěngāoxìng　　kě shí jì shang　　dāng yè gōngkàn
人 们 也 许 会 想 叶 公 看 见 真 龙 时 一 定 会 很 高 兴 。 可 实 际 上 , 当 叶 公 看

jiàn nà tiáolóngshí dùnshí bèi xià de hún fēi pò sàn　　jí mángtáozǒu le
见 那 条 龙 时 顿 时 被 吓 得 魂 飞 魄 散 , 急 忙 逃 走 了 。

From then on, people knew that Lord Ye only loved pictures or carvings that looked like dragons, but not the real thing.

cóng cǐ rénmen míngbai le yè gōng ài hào de qí shí bìng bú shì zhēn lóng   ér shì lóng de huà xiàng huò diāo kè de
从 此 人们 明 白 了 叶 公 爱好 的 其实 并 不 是 真 龙 ，而是 龙 的 画 像 或 雕刻 得

kàn shàng qù xiàng lóng de dōng xi ér yǐ   nǎi sì lóng fēi lóng zhě
看 上 去 像 龙 的 东西 而已 ，乃似 龙 非 龙 者 。

Waiting by a Stump for a Careless Hare
守株待兔

〖Waiting by a Stump for a Careless Hare〗

Once upon a time, a farmer in the State of Song was working in the field when he saw a rabbit accidentally bump into a tree stump and break its neck. The farmer took the rabbit home and cooked himself a delicious meal.

So from then on he gave up farming, and simply sat by the stump waiting for rabbits to come and run into it.

This idiom mocks those who get lucky once, and wait for it to happen again, rather than making the effort to obtain what they need.

shǒu zhū dài tù

守株待兔

cóng qián sòng guó yǒu ge zhòng tián de rén yǒu yí cì yì zhī tù zi pǎo guò lái yóu yú pǎo de tài jí
从前，宋国有个种田的人。有一次，一只兔子跑过来，由于跑得太急，

yí tóu zhuàng dào shù shàng bǎ bó zi zhuàng duàn le zhè ge rén jiǎn dào le tù zi huí jiā zuò le yí dùn měi cān
一头撞到树上，把脖子撞断了。这个人拣到了兔子，回家做了一顿美餐。

dǎ nà tiān qǐ tā gān cuì fàng xià nóng jù lián huó er yě bú gàn le měi tiān shǒu zài zhè kē shù xià děng
打那天起，他干脆放下农具，连活儿也不干了，每天守在这棵树下，等

zhe tù zi zhuàng dào shù shang
着兔子撞到树上。

zhè ge gù shì fěng cì nà xiē yīn wéi yí cì ǒu rán de xìng yùn jiù pàn zhe tā zài cì jiàng lín dào zì jǐ de tóu
这个故事讽刺那些因为一次偶然的幸运，就盼着它再次降临到自己的头

shàng ér bú zài kào qín láo zhì fù de rén
上，而不再靠勤劳致富的人。

 Rousing the Spirits with the First Drum Roll
一鼓作气

〖 Rousing the Spirits with the First Drum Roll 〗

During the Spring and Autumn Period, an army from the State of Qi confronted one from the state of Lu. After the first roll of drums from the Qi side to summon Lu to battle, the king of Lu wanted to attack. But his counselor Cao Gui suggested, "We should wait until the third drum roll, sir." As a result, the Lu army defeated the Qi army. After the battle, the king asked Cao Gui the reason for his odd advice. Cao Gui answered, "Fighting needs spirit. Their spirit was aroused by the first roll of the drums, but was depleted by the second. And it was completely exhausted by the third. We started to attack when their spirit was exhausted. That's why we won."

yì gǔ zuò qì
一鼓作气

春秋时代，齐国派兵攻打鲁国。齐军第一次击鼓以后，鲁王准备发起进攻。谋士曹刿建议等齐军击鼓三次后再进攻。结果齐军大败。战斗结束后，鲁王问曹刿为什么提出这样奇怪的建议。曹刿回答说："打仗要靠勇气。第一次击鼓，士气十分旺盛；第二次击鼓，士气有些衰落；第三次击鼓，士气就消耗尽了。敌人士气耗尽，我们发起进攻，所以取得了胜利。"

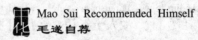 Mao Sui Recommended Himself

毛遂自荐

〚Mao Sui Recommended Himself〛

In the Warring States Period, the king of Zhao planned to ask the King of the State of Chu to resist Qin's attacks together. He sent Pingyuan to Chu to convince their king. Before Pingyuan left, a man called Mao Sui showed up, volunteered to go with him. Pingyuan said, "I haven't heard that you have any special abilities, so what help can you do over there?" Mao Sui said, "You put me in a bag, and my special abilities will stick out like an awl."

máosuì zì jiàn
毛遂自荐

战国时期，赵王想联合楚国共同抗秦。为此，他派亲王平原君到楚国游说。出发前，有一位名叫毛遂的人站出来，愿意与平原君一同前往。平原君说："我没有听过你有什么特殊的才能，跟我去能帮我干什么？"毛遂说："你把我装在囊中，我的特殊才能就像锥子那样脱颖而出了。"

So Pingyuan agreed to take Mao Sui to the State of Chu. The negotiations between the two states lasted from morning to noon, and still couldn't come to a conclusion. At this time Mao Sui came up and said, "Chu is a state big enough to rule the world. However, you are so afraid of Qin. It is such a shame that we Zhao people are embarrassed by you. Now we ask you to combine our troops, but you are acting like a coward!" The king of Chu felt ashamed after Mao Sui's passionate words. He finally agreed to send troops to fight Qin.

píngyuánjūn yú shì jiē shòu le máosuì de zì jiàn　dài tā qiánwǎngchǔguó　dào le chǔguó　píngyuánjūn yǔ
平 原 君于是接受了毛遂的自荐，带他前 往 楚国。到了楚国，平 原 君与

chǔwángtánpàn　cóngqīngchéntándào le zhōngwǔ　háiméiyǒutánpànchū ge jié guǒlái　zhèshí　máosuì
楚 王 谈判。从 清 晨谈到了 中 午，还没有谈判出个结 果来。 这时，毛遂

shàngqiánshuō　chǔguóshì dà guó　yīnggāichēng bà yú tiānxià　rán ér　nǐ gǔ zi lǐ pà qínguópà de yào
上 前说：“楚国是大国，应该 称 霸于天下。然而，你骨子里怕秦国怕得要

sǐ　lián wǒmenzhàoguórén dōugǎndàohài xiū　xiànzài　wǒmen lái lián hé nǐ menkàngqín　nǐ quèzhèbānqiè
死。 连我们赵国人都感到害羞。现在，我们来联合你们 抗秦，你却这般怯

nuò　tīng le máosuì jī áng de huà yǔ　chǔwángcánkuì le　tā zhōng yú dā yingchūbīngkàngqín
懦！ ”听了毛遂激昂的话语，楚 王 惭愧了。他 终 于答应出兵 抗秦。

This idiom describes the courage of self-recommending by people with great abilities.

xiàn zài　　máosuì　zì jiàn　　zhè jù chéng yǔ cháng yòng lái xíng róng yí　gè yǒu cái néng de rén gǎn yú xiàng bié rén
现在"毛遂自荐"这句成语常用来形容一个有才能的人敢于向别人

tuī jiàn zì　jǐ　de jīng shén hé yǒng qì
推荐自己的精神和勇气。

 Fox Basked in Tiger´s Reflected Glory
狐假虎威

〖Fox Basked in Tiger´s Reflected Glory〗

One day, a tiger found a fox and immediately caught it. The fox came up with a lie and told the tiger, "You mustn't eat me. I was sent by Heaven to rule the animals. By eating me, you will be punished by Heaven."

hú jiǎ hǔ wēi

狐假虎威

yǒu yì tiān　　yì zhī lǎo hǔ fā xiàn le　yì zhī hú li　　biàn xùn sù zhuā zhù le tā　　hú li biān chū yí gè huǎng
有一天 ，一只老虎发现了一只狐狸，便迅速抓住了它。狐狸编出一个谎

yán　duì lǎo hǔ shuō　　nǐ bù néng chī wǒ　　wǒ shì tiān dì pài dào shān lín zhōng lái dāng bǎi shòu zhī wáng de　　nǐ
言，对老虎说："你不能吃我，我是天帝派到山林 中 来 当 百 兽 之 王 的，你

yào shi chī le wǒ　huì zāo tiān qiǎn de
要是吃了我，会遭天谴的。"

The tiger couldn't completely believe the fox and asked, "What's the proof of you being the king of animals?" The fox said, "If you don't believe me, just follow me to see whether the animals are afraid of me."

lǎo hǔ duì hú li de huà jiāng xìn jiāng yí biàn wèn nǐ dāng bǎi shòu zhī wáng yǒu hé zhèng jù hú
老虎对狐狸的话将信将疑，便问："你当百兽之王，有何证据？"狐

li gǎn jǐn shuō nǐ rú guǒ bù xiāng xìn wǒ de huà kě yǐ suí wǒ dào shān lín zhōng qù zǒu yì zǒu wǒ ràng nǐ qīn
狸赶紧说："你如果不相信我的话，可以随我到山林中去走一走，我让你亲

yǎn kàn kan bǎi shòu pà bú pà wǒ
眼看看百兽怕不怕我。"

The tiger agreed, and followed the fox as it walked into the forest. The animals, seeing the tiger coming, got very scared and all ran away as fast as they could. Afterwards the fox said to the tiger proudly, "Now you see, can you find one animal that is not afraid of me?"

The tiger didn't know that it was himself who all the animals were afraid of. He believed the fox's lie.

老虎同意了并跟着狐狸一道向山林的深处走去。森林中各种兽类远

远地看见老虎来了，一个个都吓得魂飞魄散，纷纷逃命。转了一圈之后，狐

狸洋洋得意地对老虎说道："现在你该看到了吧？森林中的百兽，有谁敢

不怕我？"

老虎并不知道百兽害怕的正是它自己，反而相信了狐狸的谎言。

 Drawing a Snake and Adding Feet to It
画蛇添足

〖Drawing a Snake and Adding Feet to It〗

In the Warring States Period, a man in the State of Chu was offering a sacrifice to his ancestors. After the ceremony, the man gave a beaker of wine to his servants. The servants thought that there was not enough wine to go around and said, "Let's all draw a snake; the one who finished the picture first will get the wine. " One of them drew very rapidly. Seeing that the others were still busy drawing, he added feet to the snake.

At this moment another man finished, snatched the beaker, and drank the wine, saying,"A snake doesn't have feet. How can you add feet to a snake? "

画蛇添足

战国时期，有个楚国人祭他的祖先。祭祖仪式结束后，他拿出一壶酒赏给几个下人。下人们发现酒不够大伙喝的，就商量说："我们都来画一条蛇，谁先画好，谁就喝这壶酒。"其中有一个人很快就先画好了。但他看到同伴还没有画完，就又给蛇添上了脚。

这时，另一个人也画好了，夺过酒壶把酒喝了，并且说："蛇本来是没有脚的，你怎么能给它添上脚呢？"

 Retreating about Thirty Miles as Condition for Peace
退避三舍

〖Retreating about Thirty Miles as Condition for Peace〗

During the Spring and Autumn Period,   Duke Xian of the State of Jin Killed the crown prince Shen Sheng because he had heard slander about Shen Sheng and believed it.   He also sent his men to arrest Chong Er,   Shen Sheng's brother.   Hearing the news, Chong Er escaped from the State of Jin, remaining a fugitive for more than ten years. After innumerable hardships,   Chong Er arrived at the State of Chu at last.   King Cheng of the State of Chu treated him with high respect as he would have treated the ruler of a state, believing that he would have a bright future.

tuì bì sānshè
退避三舍

chūnqiūshíqī jìn xiàngōngtīngxìnchányán shā le tài zǐ shēnshēng yòupàirénzhuō ná shēnshēng de dì
春秋时期，晋献公听信谗言，杀了太子申生，又派人捉拿申生的弟

dì chóng ěr chóng ěr wénxùn táochū le jìnguó zài wài liúwángshí jǐ nián jīngguòqiānxīnwàn kǔ chóng
弟重耳。重耳闻讯，逃出了晋国，在外流亡十几年。经过千辛万苦，重

ěr lái dàochǔguó chǔchéngwángrènwéichóng ěr rì hòu bì yǒu dà zuòwéi jiù yǐ guójūnzhī lǐ xiāngyíng dài tā
耳来到楚国。楚成王认为重耳日后必有大作为，就以国君之礼相迎，待他

rú shàngbīn
如上宾。

King Cheng of the State of Chu gave a banquet in honor of Chong Er. Suddenly, amid the harmonious atmosphere of drinking and talking, King Cheng of the State of Chu asked Chong Er, "How will you repay me when you return to the State of Jin and become its ruler one day?"Chong Er answered, "If I should be fortunate enouge to return to the State of Jin and become its ruler, the State of Jin would be friendly to the State of Chu. If, one day, there should be a war between the two states, I would definitely order my troops to retreat thirty miles as a condition for peace. If, under that condition, you were still not reconciled, then I would fight with you."

楚成王设宴招待重耳,两人饮酒叙话,气氛十分融洽。忽然楚成王问重耳:"你若有一天回晋国当上国君,该怎么报答我呢?"重耳笑笑回答道:"要是托您的福,果真能回国当政的话,我愿与贵国友好。假如有一天,晋楚两国之间发生战争,我一定命令军队先退避三舍,如果还不能得到您的原谅,我再与您交战。"

Four years later, as might be expected, Chong Er returned to the State of Jin and became its ruler. He was the famous Duke Wen in history books. Under his management, the State of Jin became increasingly powerful. In the year 633 B.C., the Chu troops and the Jin troops confronted each other in a battle. Faithful to his promise, Duke Wen of the State of Jin ordered his troops to retreat about thirty miles before he fought back and defeated the Chu army.

四年后，重耳如期回到晋国当了国君，即历史上有名的晋文公。晋国在他的治理下日益强大。公元前633年，楚国和晋国的军队在作战时相遇。晋文公为了实现他许下的诺言，下令军队后退三十里，后来反击，大败楚军。

No More Tricks, Mr. Nan Guo
滥竽充数

〚No More Tricks, Mr. Nan Guo〛

In the Warring States Period of China, King Xuan of the State of Qi was very fond of listening to the music played on the Yu, a wind instrument. So he convened a band of more than 300 players. One of the players, Nan Guo, knew nothing about the instrument. But he managed to pass himself off by seating himself behind the other players and pretending to play.

Finally, his days were gone when the prince ascended the throne. As the latter enjoyed solo rather than harmony, each player was called in to play alone before the king. Nan Guo had to run away as fast as he could.

làn yú chōngshù
滥竽充数

战国时期，齐国的宣王喜欢听竽，就组织了一支三百人的大型吹竽乐队。这乐队里有一位南郭先生，他根本不会吹竽。但是他混在乐队里滥竽充数，每次都坐在后面，假装在与大家一起吹竽。

可是好景不长，齐宣王驾崩，王子继位。新王不喜欢听合奏而喜欢听独奏，于是，每个乐手都被叫到大王面前，一个一个吹竽。南郭先生不得不逃之夭夭。

中国传统文化经典故事100篇·英汉对照

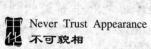 Never Trust Appearance
不可貌相

〖Never Trust Appearance〗

In the State of Zhao, there was once a scholar by the name of Gongsun Long. "I don't keep company with people who have no talents," he told his disciples. One day a man in rags came up to him, saying, "Please take me as your disciple." After looking the man up and down, Gongsun Long replied, "Tell me about your talents."

bù kě màoxiàng
不可貌相

zhàoguóyǒu ge xuézhěmínggōngsūnlóng tā céngduì dì zǐ shuō wǒ bú huì hé méiyǒuběnlǐng de rénjiāo
赵国有个学者名公孙龙。他曾对弟子说:"我不会和没有本领的人交

wǎng yì tiān yǒu ge yī shānlán lǚ de rén zǒushàngqiánduì tā shuō qǐngnínshōu wǒ zuò tú di
往。"一天,有个衣衫褴褛的人,走上前对他说:"请您收我做徒弟

ba gōngsūnlóng dǎ liang le nà rén yì fān wèndào nǐ yǒu hé běnlǐng
吧!"公孙龙打量了那人一番,问道:"你有何本领?"

"Well," said the man, "I have a loud voice which can travel very far." "Is there any-one among you who has a loud voice?" Gongsun Long asked his disciples. "No, sir!" they replied. Gongsun Long took the man as his disciple. His other disciples were laughing. "What is the use of a loud voice?" they sneered.

那人回答说："我有一个洪亮的嗓音，它能传得很远。"公孙龙问

弟子道："你们当中有没有声音洪亮的？"弟子回答说："没有。"于

是公孙龙收那人做徒弟。其他弟子窃窃私语，还嘲笑道："声音洪亮有什

么用？"

中国传统文化经典故事100篇·英汉对照

A few days later, Gongsun Long and his disciples had to make a trip to the State of Yan. They had to cross a large river. However, there was only one boat lying on the distant shore. Gongsun Long told his new disciple to prove his talent. The man readily heeded the request and yelled loudly. Very soon the boat was rowed over to ferry them all.

过了几天，公孙龙和弟子们要到燕国去。他们来到一条大河前，可是岸边却没有渡船，只有一艘停泊在远远的对岸。公孙龙就令新弟子施展其技。新弟子欣然答允，便大喊一声。很快，那艘渡船就划了过来，载他们渡河去。

Lost Axe
疑人偷斧

A man who lost his axe suspected his neighbor's son of stealing it. To him, as he observed the boy, the way the boy walked, the expression on his face, the manner of his speech, in fact everything about his appearance indicated that he had stolen the axe.

Not long afterwards, the man found his axe while digging in his cellar. When he saw his neighbor's son again, nothing about the boy's behavior or his appearance seemed to suggest that he was a thief.

疑人偷斧
yí rén tōu fǔ

一个男人丢了一把斧子，他怀疑是邻居的儿子偷的。他观察邻居的儿子，发现他的一举一动，脸上的表情，说话的方式等等都很可疑，似乎一切都在证明他就是偷斧子的人。

不久以后，这个男人在挖地窖的时候找到了他的斧子。当他再次看到邻居的儿子的时候，他的动作，外表等等看上去怎么也不像小偷的样子了。

第一部分 成语故事

 Fixing the Empty Sheepfold
亡羊补牢

〚Fixing the Empty Sheepfold〛

During the Warring States Period, King Xiang of Chu was an incapable leader. A minister named Zhuang Xin once said to King Xiang, "When you are inside the palace, minister Zhou and Xia are on your left and right sides. You all think about enjoying corrupted lives, but not caring about the administration of the state, so the state is in danger! If you don't believe me, please allow me to go to the State of Zhao to hide for a while, and see what will happen next."

wángyáng bǔ láo
亡羊补牢

zhànguóshí qī   chǔxiāngwángshí fēnhūnyōng wú dào   chǔguóyǒu yí gè dà chén   míngjiàozhuāngxīn
战国时期，楚襄王十分昏庸无道。楚国有一个大臣，名叫庄辛。

yǒu yí cì tā duìchǔxiāngwángshuō   nínzàigōng lǐ mian de shíhou   zhōuhóu hé xiàhóubànnín de zuǒyòu   nín
有一次他对楚襄王说："您在宫里面的时候，周侯和夏侯伴您的左右，您

zhěngtiānxiǎng de shì chī hē wán lè   què yì diǎn er yě bú zài hu guójiā de zhì lǐ   yīn cǐ guójiā yǐ chǔzài wēixiǎn
整天想的是吃喝玩乐，却一点儿也不在乎国家的治理，因此国家已处在危险

zhī zhōng   nín rú guǒbú xìn wǒ de huà   qǐngyǔn xǔ wǒdàozhàoguóduǒ yì duǒ   kànshì qíng jiū jìnghuìzěnyàng
之中！您如果不信我的话，请允许我到赵国躲一躲，看事情究竟会怎样。"

After Zhuang Xin left for Zhao, in merely five months, the State of Qin attacked Chu. Now thinking Zhuang Xin's words were correct, King Xiang of Chu immediately sent people to invite him back, and asked him what to do now.

zhuāng xīn dào zhào guó cái zhù le wǔ ge yuè　　qín guó guǒ rán pài bīng qīn chǔ　　zhè shí chǔ xiāng wáng cái jué de
庄 辛到 赵 国才 住了 五个 月 ， 秦 国 果然 派 兵 侵 楚 ， 这时 楚 襄 王 才 觉得

zhuāng xīn de huà bú cuò　　gǎn jǐn pài rén bǎ zhuāng xīn qǐng huí lái　　wèn tā yǒu shén me bàn fǎ
庄 辛的 话不 错 ，赶 紧 派人 把 庄 辛 请回 来 ，问 他 有 什么 办法 。

Zhuang Xin said, "The sheep has been taken away by a wolf; now it's too late to realize that the empty sheepfold should be fixed!"

庄辛说："羊已经被狼拖去了，这个时候您才想起来把空的羊圈补上恐怕为时太晚了吧！"

中国传统文化经典故事100篇·英汉对照

102

Words Heard from the Road
道听途说

〖Words Heard from the Road〗

Long ago, there were two men named Ai Zi, and Mao Kong, respectively.

Once Mao Kong said to Aizi, "Several days ago, a duck laid a hundred eggs!" Aizi didn't believe him, so he said, "Perhaps it was two ducks combined." Aizi still couldn't believe it, so Mao Kong then said, "Maybe it was three ducks." The number of ducks reached ten in the end.

dàotīng tú shuō
道听途说

cóngqián yǒuliǎng ge rén fēnbiéjiào ài zi hé máokōng
从前，有两个人，分别叫艾子和毛空。

yǒu yī cì máokōng duì ài zi shuō qián jǐ tiān yǒu yì zhī yā zi jìngrán shēng le yì bǎi ge
有一次，毛空对艾子说："前几天有一只鸭子，竟然生了一百个

dàn ài zi bú xìn máokōng yòu shuō shì liǎng zhī yā zi shēng de ài zi hái shì bú xìn máo
蛋。"艾子不信，毛空又说："是两只鸭子生的。"艾子还是不信，毛

kōng yòu shuō dà gài shì sān zhī yā zi shēng de jiù zhè yàng zuì hòu yì zhí zēng jiā dào shí zhī yā zi
空又说："大概是三只鸭子生的。"就这样，最后一直增加到十只鸭子。

After a while Mao Kong said, "Last month a piece of meat fell down from the sky, 30 zhang in length." Aizi didn't believe him, Mao Kong then said, "20 Zhang actually." Aizi still didn't belive. Later he said, "It was 10 zhang long!"

máokōngyòugàosu ài zi shuō shàng ge yuètiānshàngdiàoxià yí kuàiròu yǒusānshízhàngcháng
毛空又告诉艾子说：" 上个月天上掉下一块肉，有三十丈长。"

ài zi bú xìn máokōngshuō shì èr shízhàngcháng ài zi háishì bú xìn máokōngyòushuō
艾子不信，毛空说："是二十丈长。" 艾子还是不信，毛空又说：

shì shízhàngcháng
"是十丈长。"

Aizi asked Mao Kong, "So, as for the duck you mentioned, whose duck is it anyway? Also, about the meat that came down from the sky, where is it right now?" Mao Kong replied, "I don't know. I just heard these things from other people on the road." Aizi turned around and told his students, "Remember, words heard from the road are not to be trusted!"

艾子问毛空："你刚才说的鸭子到底是谁的？还有那块肉，掉到了什么地方？"毛空回答说："我也不知道，都是在路上听别人这么讲的。"艾子转身对着他的学生说："大家要记住像他这样道听途说，是不可信的！"

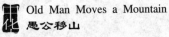
Old Man Moves a Mountain
愚公移山

〖Old Man Moves a Mountain〗

Taihang and Wangwu are two mountains, with an area of seven hundred square li and a great height of thousands of zhang.

North of the mountains lived an old man called Yugong who was nearly ninety years old. Since his home faced the two mountains, he was troubled by the fact that they blocked the way of the inhabitants who had to take a roundabout route. He gathered his family together to discuss the matter. "Let us do everything in our power to flatten these forbidding mountains so that there is a direct route to the south of Yuzhou reaching the southern bank of the Han River. What do you say?" Everyone applauded his suggestion.

yú gōng yí shān
愚公移山

<ruby>太行<rt>tài háng</rt></ruby>、<ruby>王屋<rt>wáng wū</rt></ruby><ruby>两座山<rt>liǎng zuò shān</rt></ruby>，<ruby>方圆<rt>fāng yuán</rt></ruby><ruby>七百里<rt>qī bǎi lǐ</rt></ruby>，<ruby>高数万尺<rt>gāo shù wàn chǐ</rt></ruby>。

北山住着一个名叫愚公的老人，年纪将近九十岁了。他的家门正面对

着这两座大山。愚公苦于道路阻塞，出去进来都要绕远路，便召集全家人

商量说：“我和你们尽力挖平两座大山，直通到豫州南部，到达汉水

南岸，好吗？”大家纷纷表示赞同。

Therefore Yugong took three sons and grandsons who could carry a load on their shoulders. They broke up rocks and dug up mounds of earth which were transported to the edge of the Bo Sea in baskets.

An old man called Zhisou who lived in Hequ, near a bank of a branch of the Yellow River, was amused and dissuaded Yugong, "How can you be so foolish? With your advanced years and the little strength that you have left, you cannot even destroy a blade of grass on the mountain, not to speak of its earth and stone."

愚公于是带领子孙中能挑担子的三个儿子和孙子们干了起来。凿石头，挖泥土，用箕畚运送到渤海的边上。

住在黄河支流边河曲的一个名字叫智叟的老人笑着阻止愚公说："你怎么那么傻呀，凭你的有生之年和余力，尚不能毁掉山上的草木，更不用说泥土和石头啦！"

Yugong heaved a long sigh. "Though I die, my son lives on. Sons follow sons and grandsons follow sons. My sons and grandsons go on and on without end, but the mountains will not grow in size. Then why worry about not being able to flatten them?" Zhisou of Hequ was bereft of speech.

God was moved by Yugong's sincerity and commanded the two sons of Kua'eshi to carry away the two mountains on their backs: one was put east of Shuozhou and the other south of Yongzhou. From that time onwards no mountain stood between the south of Yuzhou and the southern bank of the Han River.

愚公 长 叹 一 声 说 ："即使我死了，还有儿子在呀；儿子又 生 孙子，孙子又 生 儿子；子子孙孙没有 穷 尽的，可是山不会增高加大，何愁挖不平它们呢？"河曲智叟没有话来回答。

天帝被愚公的 诚 心感动，命令夸娥氏的两个儿子背走两座山，一座放在朔州的东部，一座放在雍州的南部。从此以后，从豫州的南部，直到汉水的南面，再也没有大山挡路了。

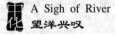

A Sigh of River
望洋兴叹

110

〖A Sigh of River〗

At the time of autumn floods when hundreds of streams poured into the Yellow River, the torrents were so violent that it was impossible to distinguish an ox from a horse from the other side of the river. Then the River God was overwhelmed with joy, feeling that all the beauty under the heaven belonged to him alone. Down the river he traveled east until he reached the North Sea. Looking eastward at the boundless expanse of water, he changed his countenance and sighed to the Sea God, saying, "As the popular saying goes, 'There are men who have heard a little about Tao but still think that no one can surpass them.' I am one of such men. "

望洋兴叹

秋汛的季节到了，无数条溪流汇入黄河，河水猛涨，河面宽得连对岸的牛马都辨不清。这样一来，河伯就洋洋自得起来了，以为世界上所有壮丽的景色都集中在自己身上了。他顺着河水向东行，一直来到北海，向东一望，一片辽阔的大海，看不见水的边际。这时，河伯才改变了他的骄傲的神态，望着海洋感慨地说："俗话说'有的人只学到万分之一的道理，就以为谁也比不上自己，我正是这样的人啊！'"

Two Concubines
逆旅二姜

〖Two Concubines〗

Yangzi went to the State of Song and spent the night in an inn. The innkeeper had two concubines. One of them was very beautiful; one of them was very ugly. The ugly one was favored; the beautiful one, on the contrary, was not favored. Yangzi asked why this was. The innkeeper replied, "The beautiful concubine considers herself very beautiful; but I certainly do not think she is beautiful. The ugly concubine considers herself very ugly; but I certainly do not think she is ugly." Yangzi said, "Disciples, remember these words, if a person can do virtuous deeds while ridding himself of any feelings of conceit, then where could he go without being welcomed?"

逆旅二妾

阳子到宋国去，住宿在旅馆里。旅馆的主人有两个姨太太，一个很美丽，另一个很丑陋。丑的受宠，美的反倒不受宠。阳子问店主为什么会是这样，店主回答说："那个美的觉得她自己很美，可是我并不感到她美；那个丑的觉得她自己很丑，可是我并不感到她丑。"阳子说："徒弟们记住这句话，要是一个人做高尚的事，又没有觉得自己很高尚的心理，那么他到哪里能不受欢迎呢？"

 Zhuangzhou Borrows Grain
庄周贷粟

〖Zhuangzhou Borrows Grain〗

Zhuangzhou's family was poor and so he went to borrow grain from Duke Jianhe, the superintendent of river-courses. The superintendent said, "All right. When I get the revenue of my fief, I will lend you three hundred yuan. Will that do?"

zhuāng zhōu dài sù
庄 周 贷 粟

庄 周家里穷得没米下锅了，不得不到监和侯那里去借粮 。监和侯说："行啊，我即将领到封邑的薪金，打算借给你三百金，可以吗？"

Zhuangzhou flushed with anger and said, "When I was on the way here yesterday, I heard someone calling me. I looked back and saw a carp in the cart-rut. I asked it, 'Come over, carp. What are you doing here?' It replied, 'I am a messenger from the East Sea. Will you save me with a bucket of water?' I said, 'All right. When I meet the princes in the State of Wu and the State of Yue, I will try to persuade them to divert the water from the West River to welcome you. Will that do?'

庄周生气得变了脸色，说："我昨天往你这里来，半路上听到有个声音在呼救，我回头一看，见到车轮碾成的沟里有一条鲤鱼，我问它说'你过来，你在这干什么啊？'鲤鱼回答说：'我是东海龙王的信使，你有一斗的水使我活下去吗？'我说'行，我将到南方去游说吴王和越王，让他们把西江的水引过来迎接你，可以吗？'

The carp flushed with anger and said, 'I have lost my normal environment and have no place to stay. I can survive with a mere bucket of water. But if you talk to me like this, you'd better look for me in the dried-fish market.' "

鲤鱼生气地变了脸色，说：'我失去了正常的生活环境，我没有地方可以活下去了，我只要获得一斗半升的水就能活命了，你竟然这么说，还不如早早地到卖干鱼的集市上去找我。'"

中国传统文化经典故事100篇·英汉对照

The Penumbras and the Shadow
罔两问影

〖The Penumbras and the Shadow〗

The penumbras asked the shadow, "A moment ago you were looking down and now you are looking up; a moment ago your hair was tied up and now it is hanging loose; a moment ago you were sitting and now you are standing; a moment ago you were walking and now you are standing still. How is all this?"

wǎngliǎngwènyǐng
罔 两 问 影

xū yǐngwènyǐng zi shuō　　　nǐ xiānqián dī zhetóuxiànzài yǎng qǐ tóu　　xiānqiánshùzhe fà jì xiànzài pī zhe
虚影问影子说："你先前低着头现在仰起头，先前束着发髻现在披着

tóu fa　　xiānqiánzuòzhexiànzài zhàn qǐ　　xiānqiánxíngzǒuxiànzài tíngxià lái　　zhèshì shénmeyuányīn ne
头发，先前坐着现在站起，先前行走现在停下来，这是什么原因呢？ "

The shadow said, "Gentlemen, why do you bother asking me such trifling questions? I do these things but I don't know why. I look like the shell of a cicada or I look like the slough of a snake. I look like the real thing, but I am not the real thing. I appear with the flame or the sun, but fade with the shade or the night.

影子回答：“君子你为什么拿这样微不足道的事情烦我呢？我就是这样地随意运动，我自己也不知道为什么会是这样。我，就如同寒蝉蜕下来的壳、蛇蜕下来的皮，跟那本体事物相似却又不是那事物本身。火光与阳光使我显现，阴暗与黑夜使我隐形。

Do I depend on the real thing? But the real thing itself has to depend on something else! When the real thing comes, I come with it; when the real thing goes, I go with it; when the real thing moves to and from, I move to and from with it. I am but moving to and from. What is there to ask about?"

我依赖有形的事物吗？而有形的事物又依赖什么呢？有形的物体到来我便随之而来，有形的物体离去我也随之而去，有形的物体徘徊不定我就随之不停地运动。这有什么可问的呢？"

Robbers Have Way

盗亦有道

〖**Robbers Have Way**〗

When one of the followers of Zhi, the Head Robber, asked him, "Do we robbers have our way of life?" Zhi answered, "How can we do away with our way of life? To guess what treasure is in the house is to be sagacious; to be the first to break into a house is to be brave; to be the last to leave the house is to be righteous; to know whether the robbery could be carried out is to be wise; to share the spoils equally is to be humane. There are no great robbers in the world who are not endowed with these five qualities."

盗亦有道
dào yì yǒudào

盗跖的门徒 向 盗跖问道："我们做 强 盗也有道吗？" 盗跖回答说：我们怎么会没有道呢？凭 空 推测屋里储 藏 着什么财物，这就是洞察力；率先进到屋里，这就是勇敢；最后退出屋子，这就是义气；能知道可否采取行动，这就是智慧；事后分配公平，这就是仁义。以上五样不能具备，却能成为大盗的人，天下是没有的。"

The Argument Above the Hao River

濠梁之辩

〖**The Argument Above the Hao River**〗

Zhuangzi and Hui Shi were strolling on the bridge above the Hao River. Zhuangzi looked into the fish in the river. "Out swim the minnows, so free and easy," said Zhuangzi "That's how fish are happy."

"You are not a fish whence do you know that the fish are happy?" Hui Shi asked.

háoliáng zhī biàn
濠梁之辩

zhuāng zǐ hé péngyǒuhuì shī zài háoshuǐ de yí zuòqiáoliángshàngsàn bù zhuāng zǐ kànzheshuǐ lǐ de cāng
庄 子和朋友惠施在濠水的一座桥 梁 上 散步。 庄 子看着水里的苍

tiáo yú shuō cāngtiáo yú zài shuǐ lǐ yōurán zì dé zhè shì yú de kuài lè a
鲦鱼说：" 苍 鲦鱼在水里悠然自得，这是鱼的快乐啊。 "

huì shī shuō nǐ bú shì yú zěn me zhī dào yú de kuài lè ne
惠施说：" 你不是鱼，怎么知道鱼的快乐呢？ "

Zhuangzi responded, "You aren't me, whence do you know that I don't know the fish are happy?"

Hui Shi said, "We'll grant that not being you I don't know about you. You'll grant that you are not a fish, and that completes the case that you don't know the fish are happy."

zhuāng zǐ shuō   nǐ bú shì wǒ   zěn me zhī dào wǒ bù zhī dào yú de kuài lè ne
庄 子 说 ：" 你 不 是 我 ， 怎么 知道 我 不 知道 鱼 的 快乐 呢 ？ "

huì shī shuō   wǒ bú shì nǐ   gù rán bù zhī dào nǐ   nǐ bú shì yú   wú yí yě méi fǎ er zhī dào yú shì bú
惠施 说 ：" 我 不 是 你 ， 固然 不 知道 你 ； 你 不 是 鱼 ， 无疑 也 没法儿 知道 鱼 是 不

shì kuài lè
是 快乐 。 "

"Let's go back to where we started when you said 'Whence do you know that the fish are happy?' you asked me the question already knowing that I knew. I knew it from up above the Hao"

zhuāng zi shuō　　　qǐng huí dào wǒ men kāi tóu de huà tí　　　nǐ wèn　　nǐ zěn me zhī dào yú kuài lè　　　zhè jù
庄 子 说 ：" 请 回 到 我 们 开 头 的 话 题 。 你 问 ' 你 怎 么 知 道 鱼 快 乐 '， 这 句

huà biǎo míng nǐ　yǐ jīng kěn dìng le　wǒ zhī dào yú de kuài lè　le　　　ér wǒ zé shì zài háo shuǐ de qiáo shàng zhī dào yú ér
话 表 明 你 已 经 肯 定 了 我 知 道 鱼 的 快 乐 了 ， 而 我 则 是 在 濠 水 的 桥 上 知 道 鱼 儿

kuài lè de
快 乐 的 。 "

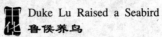 Duke Lu Raised a Seabird

鲁侯养鸟

〖Duke Lu Raised a Seabird〗

A seabird was once seen perching on the city gate of the capital of Lu.   Nobody had seen such a bird before, so they called it the "holy bird".

lǔ hóuyǎngniǎo
鲁侯养鸟

cóngqiányǒu zhī hǎi niǎo　　zài lǔ guóchéngménshang qī xī　　yīn wéi cóng lái méi yǒurén jiànguòzhè zhǒng
从 前有只海 鸟， 在鲁国 城 门 上 栖息。 因为从 来没有人见过这 种

niǎo　　suǒ yǐ rénmendōujiào tā zuò　　shénniǎo
鸟 ，所以人们都叫它做" 神鸟 "。

Duke Lu ordered his men to capture the seabird alive. They kept it in a golden cage and brought it to the Imperial Ancestral Temple. Duke Lu treated the seabird as though it were his guest of honor. Each day there would be banquets where dainties and delicacies of every kind would be offered to the seabird. Even Duke Lu's musicians had to perform for the seabird's sole amusement.

鲁侯命侍从活捉海鸟。侍从将海鸟关在金笼内，并放在太庙里供养。鲁侯视海鸟如国宾。每天都有各式各样的珍馐百味供海鸟品尝，甚至鲁侯的乐师，也要为海鸟演奏。

But the seabird was terrified by all this grandness. It became so frightened and sad that it dared not eat or drink. After three days, it died. Duke Lu thought that he had been a good host to his guest. Why not? He was treating the seabird the same way he treated himself.

<ruby>可是<rt>kě shì</rt></ruby>，<ruby>海鸟<rt>hǎi niǎo</rt></ruby><ruby>却<rt>què</rt></ruby><ruby>被<rt>bèi</rt></ruby><ruby>这些<rt>zhè xiē</rt></ruby><ruby>豪华<rt>háo huá</rt></ruby><ruby>排场<rt>pái chǎng</rt></ruby><ruby>所<rt>suǒ</rt></ruby><ruby>吓倒<rt>xià dǎo</rt></ruby>，<ruby>心里<rt>xīn li</rt></ruby><ruby>既<rt>jì</rt></ruby><ruby>惊慌<rt>jīng huāng</rt></ruby><ruby>又<rt>yòu</rt></ruby><ruby>悲痛<rt>bēi tòng</rt></ruby>，<ruby>不敢饮食<rt>bù gǎn yǐn shí</rt></ruby>，

<ruby>过了三天<rt>guò le sān tiān</rt></ruby>，<ruby>终于<rt>zhōng yú</rt></ruby><ruby>死去<rt>sǐ qù</rt></ruby>。<ruby>鲁侯<rt>lǔ hóu</rt></ruby><ruby>以为<rt>yǐ wéi</rt></ruby><ruby>他<rt>tā</rt></ruby><ruby>款待<rt>kuǎn dài</rt></ruby><ruby>海鸟<rt>hǎi niǎo</rt></ruby><ruby>已<rt>yǐ</rt></ruby><ruby>十分<rt>shí fēn</rt></ruby><ruby>周到<rt>zhōu dào</rt></ruby>。<ruby>可不是吗<rt>kě bú shì ma</rt></ruby>？<ruby>他是<rt>tā shì</rt></ruby>

<ruby>用<rt>yòng</rt></ruby><ruby>对待<rt>duì dài</rt></ruby><ruby>自己<rt>zì jǐ</rt></ruby><ruby>的<rt>de</rt></ruby><ruby>方法<rt>fāng fǎ</rt></ruby><ruby>去<rt>qù</rt></ruby><ruby>对待<rt>duì dài</rt></ruby><ruby>海鸟<rt>hǎi niǎo</rt></ruby><ruby>的<rt>de</rt></ruby>。

中国传统文化经典故事100篇·英汉对照

 Learning to Kill Dragons
屠龙之术

〚Learning to Kill Dragons〛

Zhu Pingman was a man who loved to learn. He spent a fortune in learning the skills of killing dragons from Zhili Yi. Three years later he acquired the skills of killing dragons. When he was asked what he had learned, he would be very excited demonstrating how to kill a dragon: press the dragon head, stride the dragon tail and then start killing with knife from the back. The people laughed and asked him where he could apply his skills. Suddenly he became aware that his skills were all in vain because he could find no opportunity to practice them.

tú lóng zhī shù
屠龙之术

朱萍漫是个很爱好学习的人。他变卖了家产，去拜支离益作老师，跟他学杀龙之术。转瞬三年，他学成回来。人家问他究竟学了什么，他一面兴奋地回答，一面就把杀龙的技术：怎样按住龙的头，怎样踩龙的尾巴，怎样从龙脊上开刀……，指手划脚地表演给大家看。大家都笑了问他有什么地方可以施展他的屠龙之术呢？"朱萍漫这才恍然大悟，他的本领是白学了，因为他无法找到机会去施展自己的本事。

中国传统文化经典故事100篇·英汉对照

Mr. Dongguo
东郭先生

134

【Mr. Dongguo】

Mr.Dongguo was a very kind scholar who enjoyed helping people. One day, Mr. Dongguo was walking on the road, carrying a full bag of books. Suddenly, he saw a wolf running towards him. The wolf said to Mr. Dongguo, "Help, please! Somebody wants to kill me."

So Mr.Dongguo took the books out of the bag, and let the wolf get in. Soon, a man came and asked, "Is there a wolf here?" Mr. Dongguo said, "No, there isn't."

dōngguōxiānsheng
东郭先生

东郭先生是一个仁慈的学者，很乐于助人。 一天，他背着书袋在路上走着。 忽然，从后面跑来一只狼。 狼对东郭先生说："先生，救救我吧！有人要杀我！"

于是东郭先生倒出口袋里的书，把狼藏了进去。 不一会儿，一个人找了来，问东郭先生："看见一只狼没有？" 东郭先生说："我没看见。"

135

After the man went away, the wolf cried, "Let me out!" Mr. Dongguo let the wolf out, but the wolf said, "Mr. Dongguo, I'm hungry, I must eat you!"

At this moment, a farmer came along. Mr. Dongguo told him what happened and asked him for help. However, the wolf said to the farmer, "Mr. Dongguo put me into his bag and it almost choked me. Shouldn't I eat him?"

猎人走了，狼在口袋里喊到："让我出去！"东郭先生把它放了出来。

狼嚷道："我要饿死了，东郭先生，我要吃了你！"

这时有个农夫走过来。东郭先生急忙把事情的经过告诉他，求他救命。狼却对农夫说："他把我装进口袋，差点儿把我闷死。我不应该吃他吗？"

The farmer said, "The bag is so small, you are so big, how could you fit in it?" The wolf said, "OK, let me show you." Mr.Dongguo put the wolf into the bag for the second time. The farmer said to Mr. Dongguo, "Now hurry, seal the bag and kill it with a shovel. How could you be kind to a wolf? No wolf is good."

农夫对狼说："那么小的口袋怎么能装得下你？"狼说，"好吧，我给你看看是怎么装的。"它让东郭先生再次把它装进口袋。这时农夫说："快，把口袋扎紧，用铁锹把它打死。你对狼怎么能讲仁慈？狼都不是好东西！"

中国传统文化经典故事100篇·英汉对照

138

Three at Dawn and Four at Dusk
朝三暮四

〖Three at Dawn and Four at Dusk〗

In the State of Song, there was a man who reared monkeys. He was very fond of monkeys and kept a large number of them. He had a strong bond with the monkeys; he understood them and they understood him. He loved his monkeys so much that he went as far as reducing the amount of food for his own family in order to satisfy the monkeys.

zhāo sān mù sì

朝 三 暮 四

从前，在宋国有一个养猴子的人。他非常喜欢猴子，所以养了许多，并且和它们相处得很好。他很了解猴子，猴子们也能够懂得他的意思。他非常爱他的猴子，以致于为了让猴子们吃饱，他减少了家人的粮食。

There then came a time when his family didn't have enough to eat. He had no choice but to cut down on the monkeys' food. But he was afraid that the monkeys would not submit to him. So, he decided to trick them into accepting less food. He asked them, "If I gave you three chestnuts in the morning and four in the evening, would that be enough?" The monkeys were furious and refused to accept his proposal.

bù jiǔ   tā jiā de liáng shi bú gòu chī le   tā zhǐ hǎo jiǎn shǎo le gěi hóu zi men de shí wù   dàn tā pà hóu zi
不久，他家的 粮 食不够吃了，他只好减 少 了给猴子们的食物。但他怕猴子

men shòu bu liǎo   yú shì   tā xiǎng hǒng piàn tā men jiē shòu jiǎn shǎo shí wù de xiàn shí   biàn wèn hóu zi men
们 受不了。于是，他 想 哄 骗它们接受 减 少食物的现实， 便 问猴子们：

rú guǒ zǎo shang wǒ gěi nǐ men sān ge lì zi   wǎn shang gěi nǐ men sì ge lì zi   gòu ma   hóu zi men dōu
"如果早 上 我给你们三个栗子，晚 上 给你们四个栗子，够吗？ " 猴子们都

fèn nù de biǎo shì bù tóng yì
愤怒的表示不同意。

A short while later, he asked them, "If I gave you four chestnuts in the morning and three in the evening, would that be enough?" This, the monkeys accepted and rolled around happily on the ground.

guò le yí huì er   tā yòu wèn   nà rú guǒ zǎoshang wǒ gěi nǐ men sì ge lì zi   wǎnshang gěi nǐ men sān
过了一会儿，他又问："那如果早上我给你们四个栗子，晚上给你们三

ge lì zi   zhèyàng gòu le ma   yú shì hóu zi men dōu lè de zài dì shang dǎ gǔn   hěn gāoxìng de tóng yì
个栗子，这样够了吗？"于是猴子们都乐得在地上打滚，很高兴地同意

le
了。

（左侧竖排）中国传统文化经典故事100篇·英汉对照

142

 Everything is Ready except the East Wind
万事俱备，只欠东风

〚Everything is Ready except the East Wind〛

The Story happened during the period of the Three Kindoms. Once Cao Cao from Wei led a 200,000 strong army down to the south to wipe out the kingdoms of Wu and Shu. Therefore, Wu and Shu united to defend his attack. Cao ordered his men to link up the boats by iron chains to form a bridge for the Cao's passing from the north bank of Yangtze River to the south bank. The General Commander of the allied army was Zhou Yu. He analyzed the situation carefully. Then he got a good idea. He decided to attack the enemy with fire. So he began to prepare for the coming battle. Suddenly he thought

wàn shì jù bèi   zhǐ qiàn dōng fēng
万事俱备，只欠东风

gù shì fā shēng zài sān guó shí qī   yǒu yí cì   wèi guó de cáo cāo dài le èr shí wàn jīng bīng nán xià gōng dǎ wú
故事发生在三国时期。有一次，魏国的曹操带了二十万精兵南下攻打吴

guó hé shǔ guó   zhǔn bèi xiāo miè tā men   wèi le yìng dí   wú guó hé shǔ guó jié chéng tóng méng guó   cáo jūn zhù zhā
国和蜀国，准备消灭它们。为了应敌，吴国和蜀国结成同盟国。曹军驻扎

zài cháng jiāng běi àn   cáo cāo ràng shǒu xià yòng tiě liàn jiāng zhàn chuán lián zài yī qǐ   hǎo ràng cáo jūn dù jiāng gōng dǎ
在长江北岸。曹操让手下用铁链将战船连在一起，好让曹军渡江攻打

nán àn de méng jūn   méng jūn yóu wú guó jiàng lǐng zhōu yú dài lǐng   tā zǐ xì fēn xī le xíng shì   zuì hòu jué dìng yòng
南岸的盟军。盟军由吴国将领周瑜带领，他仔细分析了形势，最后决定用

huǒ shāo diào dí rén de chuán   yú shì   tā kāi shǐ zhǔn bèi yí qiè   dāng tā jiāng yí qiè zhǔn bèi hǎo shí   fā xiàn hái
火烧掉敌人的船。于是，他开始准备一切，当他将一切准备好时，发现还

第一部分 成语故事

of the direction of wind. He needed the east wind to blow strongly in order to accomplish his scheme. However, the wind did not come for days. Thus Zhou Yu was worried about it. At that time, he got a note from Zhuge Liang, the military adviser of the State of Shu, which reads:

"To fight Cao Cao, fire will help you win.

Everything is ready, except the east wind."

<ruby>需要<rt>xū yào</rt></ruby> <ruby>东风<rt>dōng fēng</rt></ruby>。可<ruby>连续<rt>kě lián xù</rt></ruby> <ruby>几天<rt>jǐ tiān</rt></ruby>都<ruby>没有<rt>dōu méi yǒu</rt></ruby><ruby>东风<rt>dōng fēng</rt></ruby>，<ruby>周瑜<rt>zhōu yú</rt></ruby><ruby>急<rt>jí</rt></ruby><ruby>得<rt>de</rt></ruby><ruby>病倒<rt>bìng dǎo</rt></ruby><ruby>了<rt>le</rt></ruby>。<ruby>这时<rt>zhè shí</rt></ruby>，<ruby>蜀国<rt>shǔ guó</rt></ruby><ruby>的<rt>de</rt></ruby><ruby>军师<rt>jūn shī</rt></ruby><ruby>诸<rt>zhū</rt></ruby>

<ruby>葛亮<rt>gě liàng</rt></ruby><ruby>叫人<rt>jiào rén</rt></ruby><ruby>送<rt>sòng</rt></ruby><ruby>了<rt>le</rt></ruby> <ruby>一<rt>yì</rt></ruby> <ruby>张<rt>zhāng</rt></ruby><ruby>纸条<rt>zhǐ tiáo</rt></ruby><ruby>给<rt>gěi</rt></ruby> <ruby>他<rt>tā</rt></ruby>，<ruby>上面<rt>shàng miàn</rt></ruby><ruby>写着<rt>xiě zhe</rt></ruby>：

"<ruby>要<rt>yào</rt></ruby><ruby>赢<rt>yíng</rt></ruby><ruby>曹操<rt>cáo cāo</rt></ruby>，<ruby>须<rt>xū</rt></ruby><ruby>用<rt>yòng</rt></ruby><ruby>火攻<rt>huǒ gōng</rt></ruby>。

<ruby>万事<rt>wàn shì</rt></ruby><ruby>俱<rt>jù</rt></ruby><ruby>备<rt>bèi</rt></ruby>，<ruby>只<rt>zhǐ</rt></ruby><ruby>欠<rt>qiàn</rt></ruby><ruby>东风<rt>dōng fēng</rt></ruby>。"

中国传统文化经典故事100篇·英汉对照

Quickly he turned to Zhuge Liang for help. Zhuge told him not to worry and there would be an east wind in a couple of days. Two days later, the east wind helped Zhou accomplish his scheme. At last, the allied army won the war.

Later, people use it to say "All is ready except what is crucial".

zhōu yú shōu dào hòu　　lì kè xiàng zhū gě liàng qiú zhù　　zhū gě liàng jiào zhōu yú bú yào zháo jí　　liǎng tiān
周瑜收到后，立刻向诸葛亮求助。诸葛亮叫周瑜不要着急，两天

hòu　jiāng yǒu dōng fēng　guǒ rán　liǎng tiān hòu　guā qǐ dōng fēng　zhōu yú chèn zhè ge jī huì jiāng cáo jūn de zhàn
后，将有东风。果然，两天后，刮起东风。周瑜趁这个机会将曹军的战

chuán shāo huǐ　zuì hòu　cáo cāo bèi dǎ bài le
船烧毁。最后，曹操被打败了。

hòu lái　rén men yòng zhè gè chéng yǔ lái bǐ yù yàng yàng dōu zhǔn bèi hǎo le　zhǐ chà zuì hòu yí gè zhòng yào tiáo
后来，人们用这个成语来比喻样样都准备好了，只差最后一个重要条

jiàn
件。

 Showing Off One´s Skill before Lu Ban
班门弄斧

⟦Showing Off One′s Skill before Lu Ban⟧

In ancient times, Lu Ban was supposed to be a consummate master in construction and sculpture. Carpenters respect him as ancestor master. It is said that he once carved a colorful wooden phoenix that was so lifelike that it actually flew in the sky for three days. Thus it was considered the height of folly to show off one's skill with an axe in front of Lu Ban.

This idiom excoriates those who show off their slight accomplishments in front of experts.

bānménnòng fǔ
班门弄斧

cóng gǔ dài shí qǐ   lǔ bān bèi rèn wéi shì yí gè jiànzhù yǔ diāo sù fāngmiàn de yì shù dà shī   mùjiàngmen bǎ
从古代时起，鲁班被认为是一个建筑与雕塑方面的艺术大师，木匠们把

lǔ bānfèngwéi tā men de shǐ zǔ   jù shuō   tā céngjīngwéimiàowéixiào de diāo kè chū yí gè mùfènghuáng   mù
鲁班奉为他们的始祖。据说，他曾经惟妙惟肖地雕刻出一个木凤凰，木

fènghuáng xǔ xǔ rú shēngjìngránzhēn de zài tiānshàng fēi le sāntiān   shuígǎnzài lǔ bānmiànqiánmàinòngshǐ yòng fǔ
凤凰栩栩如生竟然真的在天上飞了三天。谁敢在鲁班面前卖弄使用斧

zi de jì shù   bèi rénmenrèn wéi shì shí fēnhuāngtáng kě xiào de xíngwéi
子的技术，被人们认为是十分荒唐可笑的行为。

zhè gè chéng yǔ yòng lái fěng cì nà xiē zài zhuān jiā miànqiánmàinòng de rén
这个成语用来讽刺那些在专家面前卖弄的人。

 Songs of Chu on All Sides
四面楚歌

〖Songs of Chu on All Sides〗

At the end of the Qin Dynasty (BC 221-206), the State of Chu and the State of Han fought for controlling of the country. Xiang Yu, the king of Chu, was besieged at a place called Gaixia by the Han army led by Liu Bang.   Xiang Yu was in a desperate situation, with little food and only a few soldiers.

sì miàn chǔ gē
四面楚歌

qín cháo mò nián gōng yuán qián　　　　　nián　chǔ hé hàn zhēng duó tiān xià　　chǔ wáng xiàng yǔ bèi hàn wáng
秦 朝 末 年 公 元 前 221—206 年 , 楚 和 汉 争 夺 天 下 。 楚 王 项 羽 被 汉 王

liú bāng de jūn duì jǐn jǐn de wéi kùn zài gāi xià zhè ge dì fang　　xiàng yǔ yǐ shēn chù jué jìng　liáng shi jī hū chī guāng
刘 邦 的 军 队 紧 紧 地 围 困 在 垓 下 这 个 地 方 。 项 羽 已 身 处 绝 境 , 粮 食 几 乎 吃 光

le　jiàng shì yě suǒ shèng wú jǐ
了 , 将 士 也 所 剩 无 几 。

At night, Han troops started to sing Chu folk songs. Xiang Yu was very surprised at this, and said, "Has Liu Bang occupied the whole of Chu? How can he have drafted so many Chu people into his army?" Then he fled together with the remainder of his forces.

yè lǐ hàn jūn chàng qǐ le chǔ guó de mín gē xiàng yǔ tīng le fēi cháng chī jīng de shuō hàn jūn yǐ
夜里，汉军 唱 起了楚国的民歌。 项 羽听了，非 常 吃惊地说："汉军已

jīng quán bù zhàn lǐng le zhěng gè chǔ guó de tǔ dì ma wèi shén me zài hàn jūn zhōng yǒu zhè me duō de chǔ guó rén
经 全 部占 领了 整 个楚国的土 地 吗？ 为什么在汉军 中 有这么多的楚国人

ne shuō zhe jiù cóng chuáng shàng pá qǐ lái dài zhe cán yú de shì bīng jīng huāng de táo zǒu le
呢？ "说着就从 床 上 爬起来，带着残余的士兵惊 慌 地逃走了。

This idiom is used metaphorically to mean to be in a helpless and critical situation, surrounded by the enemy on all sides."

zhè ge chéng yǔ bǐ yù sì miàn shòu dào dí rén de gōng jī　　chǔ yú gū lì wēi jí de kùn jìng
这个 成 语比喻四 面 受 到敌人的 攻击 ，处于孤立危急的困境 。

 Calling a Stag a Horse
指鹿为马

〖Calling a Stag a Horse〗

In the Qin Dynasty, the prime minister, Zhao Gao, plotted to usurp the throne. Fearing that the other ministers would oppose this, he thought of a way of testing them. He presented a deer to the emperor, and said, "This is a horse." The emperor laughed, and said, "You must be joking; this is a deer." Then Zhao Gao asked the ministers present. Some kept silent, some agreed that it was a horse, and others said that it was a deer. Later Zhao Gao had all the ministers who had said that it was a deer killed. Later, the ministers were all afraid of him.

This metaphor describes distorting facts by calling white black.

zhǐ lù wéi mǎ

指鹿为马

qín cháo chéng xiàng zhào gāo xiǎng cuàn duó dì wèi tā pà qún chén men fǎn duì tā jiù xiǎng le yí gè bàn fǎ

秦朝丞相赵高想篡夺帝位。他怕群臣们反对他，就想了一个办法

lái shì yí shì dà jiā tā qiān lái yì zhī lù xiàn gěi huáng dì shuō zhè shì yì pǐ mǎ huáng dì xiàozhe

来试一试大家。他牵来一只鹿献给皇帝说："这是一匹马。"皇帝笑着

shuō chéng xiàng nǐ nòng cuò le ba zhè shì yì zhī lù zhào gāo ràng zài chǎng de dà chén men biǎo tài tā

说："丞相你弄错了吧？这是一只鹿。"赵高让在场的大臣们表态。他

men yǒu de bú zuò shēng yǒu de gēn zhe zhào gāo shuō shì mǎ yě yǒu shuō shì lù de fán shì shuō lù de rén hòu lái

们有的不做声，有的跟着赵高说是马，也有说是鹿的。凡是说鹿的人，后来

dōu bèi zhào gāo shā le cóng cǐ yǐ hòu qún chén dōu hài pà zhào gāo

都被赵高杀了。从此以后，群臣都害怕赵高。

zhǐ lù wéi mǎ yòng lái bǐ yù gù yì diān dǎo hēi bái hùn xiáo shì fēi

"指鹿为马"用来比喻故意颠倒黑白，混淆是非。

 Going South by Driving the Chariot North
南辕北辙

〖Going South by Driving the Chariot North〗

Once a man wanted to go to the south, but his carriage was heading north. A passer-by asked him: "If you are going to the south, why is your chariot heading north?" The man answered, "My horse is good at running, my driver is highly skilled at driving a carriage, and I have enough money." The man didn't consider that the direction might be wrong; the better his conditions were, the further he was away from his destination.

The idiom "Going south by driving the chaiot North" derived from this story indicates that one's action is the opposite effect to one's intention.

nányuán běi zhé
南辕北辙

从 前 有 个 人 要 到 南 方 去 , 他 坐 的 车 子 却 向 北 方 行 驶 。 过 路 人 说 : " 你 去 南 方 , 车 子 怎 么 向 北 行 驶 呢 ? " 他 回 答 说 : " 我 的 马 很 能 跑 路 , 我 的 车 夫 驾 车 的 技 术 也 很 高 明 , 而 且 我 又 带 了 充 足 的 路 费 。 " 这 个 人 没 有 考 虑 到 方 向 弄 反 了 , 他 的 条 件 越 好 , 离 他 的 目 的 地 就 越 远 。

后 来 人 们 就 把 这 个 故 事 概 括 为 " 南 辕 北 辙 " , 比 喻 一 个 人 的 行 为 和 他 的 目 的 正 好 相 反 。

Failing to Pass an Examination
名落孙山

〖Failing to Pass an Examination〗

In the Song Dynasty (960-1279) there was a joker called Sun Shan. One year he went to take the imperial examination, and came to the bottom of the list of successful candidates. Back in his hometown, one of his neighbors asked him whether his son had also passed. Sun Shan said, with a smile, "Sun Shan was the last on the list. Your son came after Sun Shan." Later, people use this idiom to indicate failing in an examination or competition.

míng luò sūn shān
名落孙山

sòng cháo gōng yuán　　　shí yǒu yí gè míng jiào sūn shān de rén　hěn ài shuō xiào hua　yǒu yì nián
宋 朝 公 元 960 - 1279 时有一个名 叫孙山的人，很爱说笑话。有一年，

tā qù cān jiā kē jǔ kǎo shì　bǎng fā chū lái　sūn shān kǎo shàng le zuì hòu yì míng　huí dào jiā xiāng　yí wèi tóng
他去参加科举考试。榜发出来，孙山考上了最后一名 。回到家乡，一位同

xiāng xiàng tā dǎ ting zì jǐ de ér zi kǎo shàng méi yǒu　sūn shān xiào le yí xiào shuō　　sūn shān kǎo shàng zuì hòu
乡向他打听自己的儿子考上 没有 。孙山笑了一笑说："孙山考上 最后

yì míng　nín ér zi de míng zi hái zài sūn shān hòu mian ne　　　hòu lái rén men yòng　míng luò sūn shān　lái bǐ
一名 ，您儿子的名字还在孙山后面呢。"后来人们用"名落孙山"来比

yù kǎo shì méi yǒu kǎo shàng huò zhě xuǎn bá méi yǒu bèi lù qǔ
喻考试没有考 上 或者选拔没有被录取。

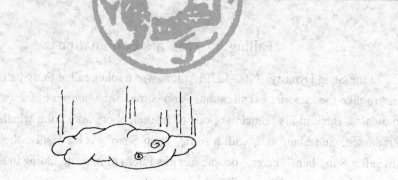

The Man of Qi Who Worried That the Sky Would Fall

杞人忧天

〖The Man of Qi Who Worried That the Sky Would Fall〗

In the Spring and Autumn Period, in the State of Qi there was a man who always let his imagination run away with him.　One day he even worried that the sky would fall on his head. He was so worried that he could neither eat nor sleep. Later, someone persuaded him that his fears were groundless, which made him felt relieved.

This idiom satirizes those who worry unnecessarily and over worried.

qǐ rényōutiān
杞人忧天

chūnqiūshídài qǐ guóyǒu yí gè xǐ huān hú sī luànxiǎng de rén yī tiān tā jìngránxiǎngdào tiānhuì
春秋时代，杞国有一个喜欢胡思乱想的人。一天，他竟然想到，天会

tā xià lái zá dào tā tóushang tā yuèxiǎngyuèhài pà zhěngtiānzuò lì bù ān chī bú xià fàn shuì bù
塌下来，砸到他头上。他越想越害怕，整天坐立不安，吃不下饭，睡不

zháojiào hòulái yǒurénnàixīn de kāidǎo tā gào sù tā tā de dānxīnshì méiyǒugēn jù de tā zhècáifàngxià xīn
着觉。后来有人耐心地开导他，告诉他他的担心是没有根据的，他这才放下心

lái
来。

qǐ rényōutiān zhè gè chéng yǔ jī xiàonà xiē háowú bì yào ér yōu lǜ guòdù de rén
"杞人忧天"这个成语讥笑那些毫无必要而忧虑过度的人。

 To Lower the Banners and Silence the Drums
偃旗息鼓

〖To Lower the Banners and Silence the Drums〗

In the Three Kingdoms Period, during a battle between Cao Cao and Liu Bei, the latter ordered his generals Zhao Yun and Huang Zhong to capture Cao Cao's supplies. Cao Cao led a large force against Zhao Yun, who retreated as far as the gates of his camp. There, he ordered that the banners be lowered and the war drums silenced, and that the camp gates be left wide open. Zhao Yun then stationed his troops in ambush nearly. When Cao Cao arrived and saw the situation, he immediately suspected a trap and withdrew his forces.

This idiom is nowadays used to indicate metaphorically halting an attack or ceasing all activities.

yǎn qí xī gǔ
偃旗息鼓

三国时代，一次曹操与刘备交战。刘备命令大将赵云、黄忠去抢夺曹操的粮食。曹操带领大军追赶赵云。赵云一直退到营寨前，叫士兵打开营门，放倒军旗，停止擂鼓，在营外设好埋伏。曹军追到，看到这种情景，怀疑有埋伏，就撤退了。

"偃旗息鼓"这个成语现在用来比喻停止攻击或者事情中止。

Like a Raging Fire
如火如荼

〖Like a Raging Fire〗

During the Spring and Autumn Period, Duke Fu Chai of Wu led a huge army against the State of Jin. He ordered his men to form three square contingents. The middle one was dressed in white and holding white flags, which looked from a distance just like the flowers of a field full of reeds. The left unit was in red and holding red flags, which looked from afar like flaming fire all over the mountains. The right unit was in black and holding black flags, which looked from a distance like thick black clouds covering the sky. Fu Chai was trying to present to the enemy a show of overwhelming force.

This idiom describes a scene of great momentum and exuberance.

rú huǒ rú tú
如火如荼

chūnqiū shí dài   wú wáng fū chāi shuàilǐng dà duì rén mǎ xiàng jìn jūn jìn jūn   tā mìnglìng jiàng shì men bǎi chéng
春秋时代，吴王夫差率领大队人马向晋军进军。他命令将士们摆成

sān gè fāng zhèn   dāng zhōng de dōu chuān bái sè yī fu   ná zhe bái sè de qí zhì   yuǎn yuǎn wàng qù jiù xiàng biàn
三个方阵。当中的都穿白色衣服，拿着白色的旗帜，远远望去就像遍

dì shèng kāi zhe bái sè tú huā   zuǒ biān de chuān hóng sè yī fu   ná zhe hóng sè de qí zhì   yuǎn yuǎn wàng qù jiù
地盛开着白色荼花。左边的穿红色衣服，拿着红色的旗帜，远远望去就

xiàng mǎn shān rán shāo zhe xióng xióng huǒ yàn   yòu biān de chuān hēi sè yī fu   ná zhe hēi sè de qí zhì   yuǎn yuǎn
像满山燃烧着熊熊火焰。右边的穿黑色衣服，拿着黑色的旗帜，远远

wàng qù jiù xiàng mǎn tiān jié jí zhe nóng mì de wū yún   fū chāi xiǎng lì yòng zhè zhǒng shēng shì qù yā dǎo duì fāng
望去就像满天结集着浓密的乌云。夫差想利用这种声势去压倒对方。

rú huǒ rú tú   zhè ge chéng yǔ xíng róng qì shì wàng shèng   chǎng miàn rè liè de jǐng xiàng
"如火如荼"这个成语形容气势旺盛，场面热烈的景象。

第一部分 成语故事

163

 Sleeping on Brushwood and Tasting Gall

卧薪尝胆

〖Sleeping on Brushwood and Tasting Gall〗

In the Spring and Autumn Period, the State of Wu defeated the State of Yue, and took the king of Yue, Gou Jian, and his wife prisoner. For several years, Gou Jian laboured as a slave in Wu. When he was released and returned to Yue, Gou Jian was determined to take revenge for losing his state. He slept on a pile of brushwood and tasted gall before every meal in order to put in mind of the shame and revenge. After ten years of careful preparations, he attacked and finally conquered the State of Wu.

This idiom is used to describe inspiring oneself to accomplish an ambition.

wò xīn cháng dǎn
卧薪尝胆

春秋时代，越国被吴国打败了。越王勾践和他的妻子都被俘虏。勾践被带到吴国做了几年的苦役。后来勾践被放回越国，他立志要报亡国之仇。从此，他每天夜里睡在柴草上面。在他住的地方，悬挂着一个苦胆，吃饭前，都要尝一尝苦胆的味道，以此提醒自己不忘过去的耻辱及仇恨。经过十年的艰苦奋斗，越国终于战胜了吴国。

"卧薪尝胆"这个成语用来形容自我激励，刻苦发奋的精神。

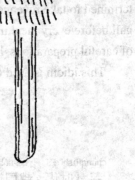

Paying Three Visits to the Cottage
三顾茅庐

In the Three Kingdoms Period, Zhuge Liang lived in seclusion in a thatched cottage of Longzhong. Liu Bei, hearing that Zhuge Liang was very knowledgeable and capable, went to visit him, taking gifts, hoping that Zhuge Liang would agree to assist him with statecraft. He had made three visits before Zhuge Liang agreed to do so, impressed by his sincerity. From then on, Zhuge Liang helped Liu Bei with all his heart, and made great achievements in both military and political spheres.

This idiom means persisting with sincerity.

sān gù máo lú
三顾茅庐

三国时，诸葛亮居住在隆中乡间的一个茅庐中。刘备听说诸葛亮很有学识，又有才能，就带着礼物去拜访他，请他出来辅佐自己打天下。刘备一共去了三次，最后才见到诸葛亮。诸葛亮见刘备十分诚恳，终于答应了他的请求。从此，诸葛亮用全部精力辅佐刘备，在军事上和政治上取得了巨大的胜利。

"三顾茅庐"这个成语用来比喻诚意与决心。

Part II Legends

第二部分
民间传说

 Wu Yan——The Ugly Concubine

丑女——无盐

〖Wu Yan——The Ugly Concubine〗

During the Spring and Autumn Period, an ugly but virtuous and strong woman became imperial concubine in a kingdom called Qi. It is said this girl was so ugly that her eyes sank deep in her face, sparse hair could hardly cover her head, and her skin was as dark as pitch. Born in Wu Yan, she was named after the place. Since she was so bad looking, she lived alone until she was 40.

丑女——无盐

春秋时期，曾有一个生得丑陋却德才出众的女子成为齐国的王后。据说这女子生来奇丑，凹眼，秃头，皮肤漆黑。她生在无盐，后人便称她"无盐"。由于她天生丑陋，所以到40岁还没有出嫁。

At that time wars surged up between the kingdoms from time to time. Civilians were encouraged by law to arrange appointment to the Emperor to give him advice. One day Wu Yan summoned up courage and went to see the Emperor Xuan. When she was presented at court, she said, "Your majesty, I would like to be at your service since our country is in great danger."

当时各国之间战争不断，黎民百姓只要对国家有好的建议，就可以直接求见国君，献计献策。有一天，无盐鼓足勇气，求见齐宣王。她来到殿前，对齐王说："陛下，我们国家正处于大危险中，我愿辅佐陛下，听从差遣！"

Emperor Xuan looked at her face and frowned. However, Wu Yan explained with confidence: "It is in a chaotic state at home with two strong kingdoms, Qin and Chu, surrounding us. But your majesty hasn't sensed the slightest danger at this moment of life and death." The emperor was struck dumb with her words. Since then he began to take more of Wu Yan's advice and gave up his luxurious life. The kingdom of Qi gradually grew prosperous as the emperor put himself in efforts to work on the government issues. Wu Yan became the emperor's concubine, known later as the famous "ugly concubine" in Chinese history books.

齐宣王见到这个丑陋的女人，禁不住皱眉。无盐却侃侃道来："秦国、楚国对齐国虎视眈眈，齐国内外交困、生死攸关，齐王您却丝毫没有意识到这一点！"齐王如同当头棒喝，猛然醒悟。从此齐王听从无盐的建议不再贪恋酒色，重新治理国家。于是齐国逐渐强大起来，而丑妇无盐也被封为王后，成为后来的史书中有名的"丑皇后"。

The Fall of a State
倾国倾城

〚The Fall of a State〛

The phrase "The Fall of a State" is used to describe the most beautiful and charming woman. The powerful emperor, Liu Che, also known as Wu Di, of the Han Dynasty was a successful sovereign. Once he heard a song written by a bandmaster in the conservatory called Li Yannian:

"In the north there is a beauty, unique among her contemporaries.

One look from her will cause the fall of a city; another, the fall of the state.

Who knows to what degree her charm can reach?"

qīngguóqīngchéng
倾国倾城

qīngguóqīngchéng shì ge chéng yǔ　yòng lái xíng róng zuì měi lì zuì wǔ mèi de nǔ rén　hàn wǔ dì liú chè shì
倾国倾城 是个成语，用来形容最美丽最妩媚的女人。 汉武帝刘彻是

yí gè hěn chéng gōng de huáng dì　yí cì　tā tīng dào le gōng tíng yuè shī lǐ yán nián zuò le yì shǒu qǔ zi
一个很成功的皇帝。一次，他听到了宫廷乐师李延年作了一首曲子：

běi fāng yǒu jiā rén　jué shì ér dú lì
"北方有佳人，绝世而独立，

yí gù qīng rén chéng　zài gù qīng rén guó
一顾倾人城，再顾倾人国。

níng bù zhī qīng chéng yǔ qīng guó　jiā rén nán zài dé
宁不知倾城与倾国，佳人难再得"。

175

The emperor was very fond of the song. He sighed, "How terrific it would be if there were a beauty like her in the world?" Soon he found that the sister of the bandmaster was just the one he was looking for. She was well educated, uniquely charming, and perfectly gorgeous. Wu Di was very excited and made her a concubine, who later was called "Mrs Li". She danced before the emperor delicately and charmingly, which Wu Di enjoyed very much.

武帝听了这首诗，叹道："世上如果真有这样的美女，那该多好啊。"很快，他发现李延年的妹妹正是他要找的美人。她不仅知书达理而且妩媚动人。武帝大喜，将这位美人招进宫来作妃子。后人称她"李夫人"。李夫人长得美丽极了，而且会唱歌、跳舞，武帝非常喜欢她。

He watched her dance attentively and finally said, "Well, my sweet beauty, the country has certainly fallen by you!" The beauty became the emperor's favorite concubine, until she passed away many years later. The idiom "The fall of a state" has been widely used by Chinese people since then.

wǔ dì rènzhēn de kànzhe tā de wǔ dǎo   zuì hòushōu   ēn   wǒ qīn ài de měirén   guó jiā dōu wèi nǐ
武帝认真地看着她的舞蹈，最后说："嗯，我亲爱的美人，国家都为你

qīngdǎo le   yì zhí dào lǐ fū rén qù shì   wǔ dì duì tā dōu jí wéi chǒng ài   qīng guó qīng
倾倒了！" 一直到李夫人去世，武帝对她都极为宠爱。 "倾国倾

chéng   de chéng yǔ diǎn gù yě jiù liú chuán kāi le
城"的成语典故也就流传开了。

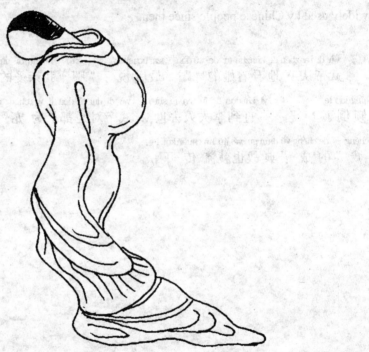

The Story of Su Liu
宿瘤的故事

〖The Story of Su Liu〗

There lived in Qi an ugly girl. Since she had a tumor in her neck, she was named Su Liu. It was goiter in fact. Because of it, people kept away from her.

sù liú de gù shì
宿瘤的故事

zài qí guó zhù zhe yí gè chǒu nǚ　　yīn wéi qí jǐng xiàng xià zhǎng le yí gè dà liú zi　　suǒ yǐ dà jiā jiù chēng tā
在齐国住着一个丑女，因为其颈项下长了一个大瘤子，所以大家就称她

sù liú nǚ　　dàn shí jì shàng shì gè zhǒng wù　　rén men yīn cǐ ér shū yuǎn tā
宿瘤女。但实际上是个肿物。人们因此而疏远她。

Once Emperor Min went on a sightseeing tour to the suburbs. All the people crowded along the road while Su Liu concentrated on picking mulberry leaves. As she was called before the emperor, she explained she was doing her job wholeheartedly and not noticing anything else.

一次齐愍王出游，前呼后拥，车骑威盛，男女老幼都聚集路旁，而宿瘤女却继续在路旁采桑，对齐愍王的出巡视若无睹。当宿瘤女被叫到齐愍王面前问其究竟时，她回答说她在专心致志地采桑，不曾留意其他的事情。

Emperor Min thought her a virtuous woman and wanted to take her back. And unexpectedly, she refused and said she should ask her parents' permission first. The emperor respected her will and held a grand marriage for her. Later she assisted in governing the country and brought peace and prosperity to people.

mǐn wáng rèn wéi tā shì bù kě duō dé de xián shū nǚ zǐ　　zhǔn bèi zài tā huí gōng　　bú liào què zāo dào sù liú nǚ
愍 王 认为她是不可多得的贤淑女子，准 备载她回 宫 ，不料却遭到宿瘤女

de jù jué　　sù liú nǚ shuō zhè yàng de shì tā yīng xiān bǐng míng fù mǔ zài zuò shāng liang　　qí mǐn wáng wán quán zūn
的拒绝。宿瘤女说这样的事她应 先 禀 明父母再做 商 量 。齐愍王完全尊

zhòng tā de yì yuàn　　wèi tā jǔ xíng le shèng dà de hūn lǐ　　hòu lái　　sù liú nǚ fǔ zuǒ qí mǐn wáng guǎn lǐ cháo
重 她的意愿 ， 为她举行了 盛 大的婚礼。 后来 ，宿瘤女辅佐齐愍王 管理朝

zhèng　　gěi guó jiā hé rén mín dài lái le chāng shèng yǔ fán róng
政 ，给国家和人民带来了 昌 盛 与繁荣。

中国传统文化经典故事100篇·英汉对照

 Battle at the Fei River
淝水之战

〖Battle at the Fei River〗

The story happened in 383 AD. King Fu Jian of Qin in North China led an army of 870,000 men to invade the State of Jin. Jin only had three generals, to lead 80,000 warriors to resist the invaders.

In November, the enemy reached the Fei River in Jin territory and began to set up defenses at the riverside. This later became the famous "Battle at the Fei River."

Across the river was Jin's troop. Jin's general Xie Xuan, as he realized there was a great disparity of strength, came up with a strategy. They sent a herald to take a message

淝水之战

公元 383 年，中原北部的秦王苻坚带领 87 万大军攻打晋国，而晋国只有 3 位将军率领 8 万晋军抵抗。

11 月秦军打到晋国领土的淝水岸边，并开始在岸边建立防护设施，这就是著名的"淝水之战"。

晋军大将谢玄见秦军在淝水驻扎，意识到两军势力悬殊，便想到一

第二部分 民间传说

183

to Fu Rong, King Fu Jian's major general, that said, "You are setting up defenses along the river, so it is quite obvious that you are planning for a long war. But as you are far from your country and supplies cannot be timely guaranteed, you are no doubt putting yourselves in a very disadvantageous situation. Why don't you let your troop retreat a few hundred yards so that we can cross the river to fight a decisive battle with you?"

This message was taken to King Fu Jian. He laughed and said, "How silly those generals are! How dare they wade across the river to fight against a troop of 870,000 men! They surely overrate themselves. Let's retreat so that they can come across. While they are still tired from the crossing, we will wipe them out with ease."

个取胜的策略，就派使者去见秦军大将苻融，对他说："你们在河岸驻守

很明显是打算打一长仗，但是你们远道而来，粮草也不一定能供应得

上，你们这不是把自己处于不利的地位？不如你们退后一些，我军过河，在地面

上公平地打一仗如何？"

谢玄傲慢的态度让苻坚哈哈大笑，说：多么傻的士兵啊！晋军少我

们人数十倍，竟然如此不自量力。 好！我就将计就计，稍向后退，待

晋军刚渡过河还在疲劳的时候，将他们一举消灭。

The retreat started. In a few seconds, there suddenly came a roaring cry of Jin warriors from behind, "The king is defeated!" As the purpose of the action had not been properly declared, many men mistakenly believed that they were truly defeated. Therefore, they ran faster until the whole troop became beyond control.

A small troop of 8000 Jin warriors immediately crossed the river and attacked the enemy from behind. General Fu Rong attempted to give a counterattack, but it was too late. His troop was already in a thorough confusion and no one would obey his order. Qin's army of 870,000 was defeated by Jin's general Xie's strategy. "The Battle of Fei River" became a famous miracle event in Chinese war history, as 80,000 men beat 870,000 men.

于是符融答应了谢玄的要求，指挥秦军后退。这时突然听到晋军的人马在秦军阵后大叫："秦兵败了！秦兵败了！"秦军正好接到撤退的命令，信以为真，转眼间士气一落千丈，失去了控制，转身竞相奔逃。

这时谢玄率领8千多骑兵，渡过河来，向秦军发起了猛攻。大将符融试图反击却已经来不及了。士兵们晕头转向，没有人再听他的命令，结果秦兵溃不成军。晋军凭借一个诱敌撤退的计策，不费力气地以8万兵马战胜了87万敌军。"淝水之战"成为了中国历史上著名的以少胜多的战役。

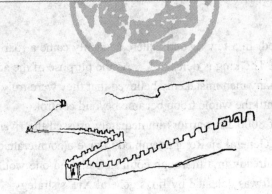

186

 Lady Meng Jiang Wailed at the Great Wall
孟姜女哭长城

〖Lady Meng Jiang Wailed at the Great Wall〗

The story of Lady Meng Jiang has been passed down in China from generation to generation. It happened during the Qin Dynasty. At that time, the government, ruled by Emperor Qin Shihuang, ordered the draft of building the Great Wall. Many young men were taken unwillingly to the construction site and forced to do restless hard work, until exhausted to death.

mèngjiāng nǚ kū chángchéng
孟 姜 女 哭 长 城

mèngjiāng nǚ de gù shi zài zhōngguóbèi yí dài yí dài de chuánsòngxià lái　　zhè ge gù shì fā shēngzài qíncháo
孟 姜 女的故事在 中 国被一代一代地 传 颂下来 。 这个故事发 生 在秦 朝

shí hou 　 nà shí houqín shǐ huángzhèngxiūzhùwàn lǐ chángchéng 　 guān fǔ dàochù qù zhuāniánqīng de nán zǐ yòngzuò
时候 ，那时候秦始 皇 正 修筑万里长 城 。官府到处去抓 年轻的男子用作

míngōng 　　 bèizhuā qù de rén bù fēnbáitiānhēi yè de xiūzhùchángchéng 　 bù zhī lèi sǐ le duōshǎo
民工 。 被 抓 去的人不分白天黑夜地修筑 长 城 ，不知累死了多少。

In the city of Suzhou, there was a beautiful young lady named Meng Jiang. One late afternoon, she was doing housework in her parents' garden when she was startled by a young man who leapt over the fence. Panting violently, he apologized for the unintended intrusion. He told Meng Jiang that his name was Fan Xiliang. He had been escaping from the Great Wall draft and exhausting from fatigue and hunger. Meng Jiang's family showed great sympathy for Fan Xiliang's situation, and invited him to stay with them.

苏州城有个美丽的女子，名叫孟姜女。一天傍晚，她正在自家的院子里做家务，突然一个男子翻墙而入，吓了她一大跳。只见那个人恳求道："别喊，救救我吧！我叫范喜良，是来逃难的。"孟姜女的父母见他又冻又饿，就把他收留下来。

Eventually, the handsome, good-mannered young man and the dexterous pretty young woman fell in love. Meng Jiang's parents were so glad that their beloved daughter had found a great groom and planned to have them married.

However, only three days after Meng Jiang and Fan Xiliang's wedding, local authorities broke in their house. Fan Xiliang was caught and sent to the Great Wall construction site in the far north of China.

jiànjiàn de yīngjùnxiāosǎ de fàn xǐ liáng yǔ měi lì wēnróu de mèngjiāng nǚ xiāng hù chǎnshēng le ài mù zhī
渐渐地， 英俊潇洒的范喜良与美丽温柔的孟 姜 女 相互产 生了爱慕之

xīn xīn ài de nǚ ér zhǎodào le rú yì de lángjūn mèngjiāng nǚ de fù mǔ qīn shí zài tài gāoxìng la mángzhewèi
心。心爱的女儿找 到了如意的郎君， 孟 姜 女的父母亲实在太高兴啦， 忙 着为

tā mencāobànhūn lǐ
他们操办婚礼。

rán ér hūnhòugāngsāntiān yá yì chuǎngjìn mén lái yìng bǎ fàn xǐ liángzhuāzǒu qù běifāngxiūcháng
然而婚后 刚 三天，衙役 闯 进门来， 硬把范喜良抓走，去北方修 长

chéng qù le
城 去了。

Lady Meng Jiang waited day and night for her husband to return. She finally decided to set off to look for him. Saying farewell to her parents, she started her long journey to the Great Wall. After conquering countless obstacles on the way, she arrived in the construction site one day. However, she could not find her husband Fan Xiliang there. Eventually bad news came that Fan Xiliang had already died of exhaustion and was buried in the Great Wall, among thousands of other workers.

孟姜女日夜盼着丈夫回来，她决定自己到长城去找他。于是孟姜女告别了父母，上路了。一路上，也不知经历了多少磨难。终于，凭着顽强的毅力，她到达了长城，却始终不见丈夫的踪影。最终，她得知丈夫已经累死，与成千上万的民工一样葬在长城脚下。

中国传统文化经典故事100篇·英汉对照

Lady Meng Jiang could not help crying and crying.　Deep sorrow filled her heart and she did not stop wailing for three days and three nights.

All of a sudden, with a tremendous noise, a section of the Great Wall, several hundred miles in length,　collapsed over her bitter wail,　revealing a great number of bodies and bones.　Meng Jiang's tears dropped onto her husband's dead body as she recognized it.　She finally found him,　but he could never see her again.　She hugged his body and went to the nearby shore of BoHai.　After saying farewell for the last time to her beloved husband in her mind, she jumped into the sea.

猛地听到这个噩耗，孟姜女大哭起来，她悲痛欲绝，整整哭了三天三夜。

突然，在孟姜女悲愤的哭声之中，伴随着一声巨响，长城倒塌了一大段，有几百里长，断墙下面露出数千具尸骨来。孟姜女最终认出了丈夫的尸体，泪水洒满了范喜良的尸骨。她终于找到了丈夫，他却再也见不到她了。她抱着丈夫的尸体向渤海边走去，内心默默向他做最后的道别，纵身跳入大海中。

Never Stop Half Way

乐羊子求学

〖Never Stop Half Way〗

In the Warring States Period, a man called Yue Yangzi lived in the State of Wei. His wife was very angelic and virtuous, who was loved and respected dearly by the husband. Yue Yangzi was convinced by his wife to go to a distant place to study classics with a talent teacher, leaving his wife home alone. Even though missing her husband deeply, Yue Yangzi's wife was willing to sacrifice it for her husband's career.

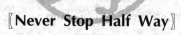

yuèyáng zǐ qiú xué
乐羊子求学

zhànguóshí qī wèiguóyǒu ge jiàozuòyuèyáng zǐ de rén yuèyáng zǐ de qī zi bù jǐn zhī shū dá lǐ ér qiě
战国时期，魏国有个叫作乐羊子的人。乐羊子的妻子不仅知书达理而且

qín láo xián huì suǒ yǐ yuèyáng zǐ duì tā hěnjìngzhòng zài qī zi de quànshuōxià yuèyáng zǐ shōu shi hǎo
勤劳贤惠，所以乐羊子对她很敬重。在妻子的劝说下，乐羊子收拾好

xíng li chū yuǎnmén qù qiúxué yuèyáng zǐ zǒuhòu qī zi hěnshì sī niànzhàng fu dàn tā bǎzhèfèn sī niàn
行李，出远门去求学。乐羊子走后，妻子很是思念丈夫，但她把这份思念

mái zài xīn dǐ wèi le zhàng fu de xué yè ér mò mòfèngxiànzhe
埋在心底，为了丈夫的学业而默默奉献着。

One day, his wife was weaving on the loom. She suddenly heard a knock on the door. Surprisingly, it was Yue Yangzi. At his coming, the wife was very excited. She asked, "Why have you come back so soon? Have you finished with your studies?" The husband said, "No, I haven't, but I have missed you so much that I had to drop it to come back and be with you." The wife got very disappointed. She suddenly picked up a pair of scissors and cut down what she had woven on the loom, which made Yue Yangzi very puzzled. His wife declared, "If something is stopped halfway, it is just like the cut cloth on the loom. The cloth will only be useful if it is finished. But now, it has been nothing but

一天，妻子正在织布，忽然听见有人敲门，站在面前的竟然是乐羊子，见到自己日夜想念的丈夫，妻子很高兴，问道："这么快就回来了，你已经学成了？"乐羊子望着妻子，回答说："没有，只是因为太想念你了，所以不得不中途回来看你。"妻子听了非常失望。突然她抓起剪刀，走到织布机前，把织了一大半的布都剪断了。乐羊子对此困惑不解。妻子说："如果做什么都半途而废，那就像机杼上剪断的布一样。布只有织成布匹才会有用。而现在它乱七八糟，什么都不是，这正像你的学业一

中国传统文化经典故事100篇·英汉对照

a mess, and so it is with your study."

Yue Yangzi was greatly moved by his wife. He left home resolutely and went on with his study. He didn't return home to see his beloved wife until gaining great achievements seven years later.

yàng   yì wúsuǒchéng
样 ，一无所 成 。"

yuèyáng zǐ tīng le zhèhuà   huǎngrán dà wù   tā zài cì lí kāi jiā qù qiúxué   zhěngzhěngguò le qī niáncái
乐羊子听了这话， 恍 然大悟。 他再次离开家去求学， 整 整 过了七年才

zhōng yú xué yè yǒuchéng   zhè cái huí dào jiā zhōng yǔ qī zi tuán jù
终 于学业有 成 ，这才回到家 中 与妻子团聚。

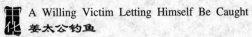

A Willing Victim Letting Himself Be Caught
姜太公钓鱼

〖A Willing Victim Letting Himself Be Caught〗

The story happened around 3000 years ago.　There was a wise man named Jiang Ziya living in a village near the Weishui River. He often went fishing at the Weishui River, but he would fish in an unusual way. He hung a straight fishhook, without bait, three feet above the water.

jiāng tài gōng diào yú
姜太公钓鱼

gù shi fā shēng zài　　　　duōniánqián　　yǒu ge zhì zhě míng zi jiàojiāng zǐ yá　zhù zài wèishuǐ hé biān de
故事发生在3000多年前。　有个智者名字叫姜子牙，住在渭水河边的

xiǎocūnzhuāng lǐ　　tā chángzài wèi hé biāndiào yú　bú guò　tā diào yú de fāng fǎ hěn tè bié　tā yòngzhí gōu
小村庄里。他常在渭河边钓鱼，不过，他钓鱼的方法很特别，他用直钩

diào yú　　yú gōushàng yě méiguà yú ěr　ér qiě yú gōu lí shuǐmiànháiyǒusānchǐ yuǎn
钓鱼，鱼钩上也没挂鱼饵，而且鱼钩离水面还有三尺远。

One day a farmer named Wu Ji went to the river, and saw the strange way of fishing by Jiang Ziya.　He laughed and said,　"How stupid it is to even think about fishing this way, how many fishes can you get?" Jiang Ziya replied, "If a fish doesn't want to live any more, it will come and swallow the hook itself."

yì tiān　　yí gè jiào wǔ jí de qiáo fū　lù guò hé biān　　kàn dào jiāng zǐ yá qí tè de diào yú fāng fǎ　　xiào
一天，一个叫武吉的樵夫路过河边，看到姜子牙奇特的钓鱼方法，笑

dào　　xiǎng chū zhè zhǒng fāng fǎ diào yú zhēn shì tài chǔn le　　nǐ zhè yàng néng diào duō shǎo yú ne　　　jiāng zǐ
道："想出这种方法钓鱼真是太蠢了，你这样能钓多少鱼呢？"姜子

yá dá dào　　rú guǒ yú ér bù xiǎng huó le　　zì rán huì shàng gōu de
牙答道："如果鱼儿不想活了，自然会上钩的。"

Soon his strange way of fishing was reported to Ji Chang, the Count of the feudal estate. Ji Chang was very interested, and went to visit Jiang personally. Soon they became great friends as Ji Chang realized that Jiang might be a great talent. He invited Jiang to work for him. Jiang helped Ji Chang and his son turn over the Shang Dynasty and establish the Zhou Dynasty. Jiang was given the title of Taigong, so people called him "Jiang Taigong".

Today, people use this old idiom "A Willing Victim Letting Himself Be Caught" to describe someone who willingly falls in a trap or does something regardless of the result.

后来有人将姜子牙用直钩钓鱼的事报告给诸侯姬昌，姬昌觉得很有趣。姬昌亲自来拜访姜子牙，跟他交了朋友。姬昌认为姜子牙会成为了不起的人物，遂邀请他为自己工作。后来姜太公辅佐文王，继而辅佐文王的儿子武王，灭了商朝，建立了周朝。姜子牙被封为太公，人们都称他为"姜太公"。

今天，人们用"姜太公钓鱼，愿者上钩"这个成语形容自投罗网的人。

中国传统文化经典故事 100 篇·英汉对照

200

Dead Horse for 500 Gold
五百金买死马

〖Dead Horse for 500 Gold〗

During the Warring States Period, the State of Yan was defeated by the State of Qi. When King Zhao was crowned as the king of Yan, he was determined to make the state prosperous. One day, he said to Guo Wei, a minister, "Can you tell me how I can get great talents to help me make my state strong?" Guo Wei replied by telling a story, "Once there was a king who offered a thousand ounces of gold for a winged steed, a horse which can run 1000 kilometers a day. He sent one of his men to search through the

wǔ bǎi jīn mǎi sǐ mǎ
五百金买死马

zhàn guó shí dài　　yān guó bèi qí guó dǎ bài hòu　　yān zhāo wáng dēng shàng yān guó wáng wèi　　měi rì lǐ xiǎng de
战国时代，燕国被齐国打败后，燕昭王登上燕国王位，每日里想的

jiù shì rú hé ràng guó jiā chāng shèng qǐ lái　　yí cì zhāo wáng duì chéng xiàng guō wéi shuō　　nǐ néng gào sù wǒ
就是如何让国家昌盛起来。一次昭王对丞相郭隗说："你能告诉我

zěn yàng cái néng qiú dé néng bāng zhù wǒ qiáng guó xìng bāng de rén cái ne　　　　guō wéi jiǎng le xià mian de gù shi
怎样才能求得能帮助我强国兴邦的人才呢？"郭隗讲了下面的故事：

céng jīng yǒu yí wèi guó wáng　　xiǎng yòng yì qiān liǎng jīn zi mǎi qiān lǐ mǎ　　biàn pài shǒu xià de rén dào quán guó gè
"曾经有一位国王，想用一千两金子买千里马，便派手下的人到全国各

country, but the man only brought back the head of a dead steed for half of the gold. The king got outraged. However, the man said, 'When people learn that you have paid so much for a dead horse, they will certainly offer to sell you a steed if anyone has got one. As was expected, the king got three steeds in less than a year. If you are sincerely seeking top talents, why don't you treat me as a dead horse of that sort now?'"

chù xún zhǎo nà rén què zhǐ zhǎo huí yì pǐ sǐ mǎ de tóu guó wáng fēi cháng shēng qì kě nà rén jiě shì shuō
处寻找，那人却只找回一匹死马的头，国王非常生气。可那人解释说：

rén men tīng shuō le nín mǎi sǐ mǎ dōu huā wǔ bǎi jīn ruò yǒu qiān lǐ mǎ yí dìng huì zhēng zhe mài gěi nín de jié
'人们听说了您买死马都花五百金，若有千里马一定会争着卖给您的。结

guǒ bù chū suǒ liào bú dào yì nián guó wáng dé dào sān pǐ qiān lǐ mǎ xiàn zài dà wáng guǒ zhēn xiǎng yào zhāo lǎn rén
果不出所料，不到一年，国王得到三匹千里马。现在大王果真想要招揽人

cái nà jiù bǎ wǒ dāng chéng nà pǐ sǐ mǎ ba
才，那就把我当成那匹死马吧！'"

King Zhao built Guo Wei a very expensive villa and regarded him as a teacher. Soon his sincerity was spread to every corner of the land. In a couple of years, great talents such as Yue Yi, Zou Yan, all came from different states to work for King Zhao. Very soon, with the assistance of these political and military talents, Yan became a powerful state and eventually invaded Qi. As Qi was defeated, King Zhao accomplished his dream of revenge.

于是昭王为郭隗建造了豪华的别墅，并拜郭隗为师。很快，昭王招贤纳士的诚意传开了。几年之中，像乐毅、邹衍这样的人才争相来到燕国。在这些政治和军事人才的辅佐下，燕国逐渐强盛起来，于是发兵攻打齐国，结果齐军大败。燕昭王终于报了仇雪了恨。

Bian He's Jade

卞和泣玉

〖Bian He's Jade 〗

This story happened in the Spring and Autumn Period.   A man in the State of Chu, named Bian He, found a rough jade on Mount Chu. He decided to present the valuable jade to the emperor to show his official loyalty to his sovereign, Chuli. Unluckily, the jade was judged as a common stone by the court jaders, which made Emperor Chuli very angry, and had Bian He's left foot cut down cruelly.

biàn hé qì yù
卞和泣玉

zhè ge gù shi fā shēng zài chūn qiū shí qī　　　yí gè jiào biàn hé de　chǔ guó rén zài chǔ shān zhōng zhǎo dào yí kuài
这个故事发 生 在 春 秋时期 。一个叫卞和的 楚国人在楚 山 中 找到一块

pú yù 　　tā jué dìng jiāng zhè kuài pú yù xiàn gěi lì wáng 　yǐ shì tā de zhōng chéng　　bú xìng de shì 　zhè kuài pú
璞玉 ，他决定 将 这块璞玉献给厉 王 ，以示他的 忠 诚 。 不幸的是 ，这块璞

yù bèi jiàn dìng chéng pǔ tōng de shí tou 　lì wáng hěn shēng qì 　　mìng rén cán rěn de kǎn diào le tā de zuǒ jiǎo
玉被鉴定 成 普通的石头 。 厉王很 生 气 ，命人残忍地砍掉了他的左脚 。

After the enthronement of the new emperor Chuwu, Bian He decided to submit the jade to Chuwu to clarify matters. Emperor Chuwu also had it checked by the jaders in the court. The conclusion was the same and Bian He lost the other foot.

After the death of Emperor Chuwu, the prince Chuwen was enthroned. One day, he heard that a man in his state, named Bian He, had been crying his heart out on a hill for days and nights. He ordered his men to find out why he was so sad. Bian He sobbed out, "Call a spade a spade. Why was a real jade mistaken as a plain stone again and again? Why was a loyal man thought faithless time and time again?"

厉王死后，武王即位。卞和又捧着他的璞玉去献给武王。武王叫玉工鉴定，结果还是被鉴定成一块普通的石头。武王命人又砍掉了他的右脚。

武王死后，文王即位。一天，文王听说有个叫卞和的，在山脚下整日整夜地痛哭不止。文王觉得奇怪，派人去问他如此伤心的原因。卞和泣不成声地说："是什么就是什么，为什么总是把宝玉说成是石头？为什么总是把诚实的人说成是骗子？"

Emperor Chuwen was touched by Bian He's deep grief and ordered the jaders to open the "stone" to have a close look. To their astonishment, in the rough coat, the pure content was sparkling and translucent. Then it was carefully cut and polished fine and at last the jade became a rare treasure of the State of Chu. In memory of the faithful man Bian He, the emperor named the jade by Bian He.

wénwáng bèi biàn hé de zāo yù gǎndòng le　　jiù mìng yù gōng jiāng shí tou pōu kāi　　zǐ xì jiàndìng　　lìng tā men
文 王 被 卞和的 遭 遇 感 动了，就 命 玉 工 将 石头剖开，仔细鉴 定 。令他们

dà chī yī jīng de shì zài cū cāo de wài biǎo xià　　yí kuài bǎo yù yì yì shēnghuī　　jīngyíng tī tòu　　tā bèi xiǎo xīn yì
大吃一惊的是在粗糙的外 表 下，一 块 宝玉熠熠 生 辉，晶 莹 剔透 。它被小心翼

yì de qiē gē　　pāoguāng　　zhōng yú zhè kuài pú yù chéngwéi chǔ guó de　xī shì zhēnbǎo　　hòu lái wénwáng bú wàng biàn
翼地切割 、抛 光 ，终 于这块璞玉 成 为楚国的稀世珍宝。后来文 王 不忘卞

hé de gōngláo　　bǎ zhè kuài bǎo yù mìngmíngwéi　　hé shì bì
和的 功劳，把这块宝玉命 名 为 " 和氏璧 " 。

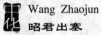

Wang Zhaojun

昭君出塞

〖**Wang Zhaojun**〗

Known as one of the "Four Greatest Beauties" in Chinese history, Wang Zhaojun was a court lady in the Han Dynasty, married off a Khan of the Xiongnus, a nomadic people to the north. Even though a number of such women were married in the interests of diplomacy at that time, Wang Zhaojun stood out as the only one who chose to do so herself.

昭君出塞

在中国历史上被称为"四大美女"之一的王昭君原是汉朝的宫女。她嫁给了北部的牧民、匈奴人的可汗。尽管与匈奴和亲的女子有很多,可王昭君却是惟一一个志愿嫁出去的汉女。

In the year 33 BC, the Xiongnus wanted to establish friendly relations with the Han Dynasty. The Khan came to the Han capital Chang'an personally and requested a Han princess as a bride. This was a way of cementing relations frequently used in those days. Han Emperor Yuan Di said he would send one of his imperial court ladies and give her away like his own daughter. He asked for volunteers. The idea of leaving their homeland and comfortable life at the court for the grasslands of the far and unknown north was unacceptable to most of the young women. But not to Wang Zhaojun: she saw it as a chance to leave the empty palace life and possibly play a more important role than she ever would in Chang'an. She applied.

公元前33年，匈奴人想与汉朝建立亲善关系。可汗亲自来到汉
朝的首都，长安，请求汉元帝将公主许配给他。在当时，用这种方
法促进两国和亲是很普遍的事情。汉元帝说他将选送一个宫女，像嫁
亲生女儿一样将她嫁给单于。他问有谁愿意前往。对于多数妇女来
说，离开自己的家乡和舒适的皇宫生活，到遥远未知的北方草原都是
难以接受的事情。王昭君却不然，她将其看作是离开皇宫生活并且
可能会比在长安发挥更大作用的机会。她答应前往匈奴和亲。

The Kahn was very happy about getting such a beautiful lady as his wife. Saying farewell to her hometown and palace, Wang Zhaojun left to begin a new life in the far north. It took a very short time for her to get used to the new environment, as the Xiongnu people showed respect to their new queen.

Wang Zhaojun convinced her husband to stay peaceful with the Han, as she introduced Han culture and traditions to the Xiongnus. Due to Wang Zhaojun's efforts, the Xiongnu and the Han never had a war in the next sixty years.

qǔ dào zhè yàng yī wèi piàoliang de gōngzhǔ zuò qī zi   kè hán fēi cháng gāoxìng   wáng zhāojūn gàobié le
娶到这样一位漂亮的公主作妻子，可汗非常高兴。 王昭君告别了

gù xiāng hé huánggōng   zài yáoyuǎn de běifāng kāishǐ le quánxīn de shēnghuó   tā hěn kuài shìyìng le xīn de
故乡和皇宫，在遥远的北方开始了全新的生活。她很快适应了新的

huánjìng   xiōng nú rén duì zhè wèi xīn huánghòu fēi cháng jìngzhòng
环境，匈奴人对这位新皇后非常敬重。

wáng zhāojūn jiāng zhōngyuán de wénhuà yǔ chuántǒng jiè shào gěi xiōng nú   tā shuì fú zhàng fu yǔ hàncháo
王昭君将中原的文化与传统介绍给匈奴，她说服丈夫与汉朝

bǎo chí yǒu hǎoguān xì   yóu yú wáng zhāojūn de nǔ lì   xiōng nú yǔ hàncháo hé mù xiāng chǔ   zài hòu lái de
保持友好关系。由于王昭君的努力，匈奴与汉朝和睦相处，在后来的

liù shí nián lǐ cóngwèi fā shēng guò zhànzhēng
六十年里从未发生过战争。

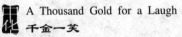

A Thousand Gold for a Laugh

千金一笑

〖A Thousand Gold for a Laugh〗

The story happened in 782 B.C., King You of Zhou was very corrupt. His minister Bao Xiang tried to remonstrate him, but he got angry and put Bao Xiang in jail. In order to rescue Bao Xiang, his son purchased the beautiful Bao Si and traded her for the minister. Since King You had Bao Si, he became even more negligent of state affairs, spending all his time with Bao Si. However, one thing about Bao Si made him unhappy: she never smiled.

qiān jīn yí xiào

千金一笑

这个故事发生在公元前782年。周幽王昏庸无道，大臣褒响来劝谏，但被周幽王一怒之下关进监狱。为了救出父亲，褒响的儿子将美女褒姒献给周幽王，周幽王这才将褒响释放。周幽王有了褒姒，从此不再关心朝政，整日让褒姒陪伴左右。不过，有一件事让周幽王很不开心，那就是褒姒从来不笑。

A sycophant minister came up with an idea: lighting the beacon towers on top of Mount Li and make a fool of all the vassal states. The beacon towers were used to send signals when the guards saw an invasion coming toward the Zhou State. King You took this idea and lit up all the beacon towers. The army generals thought there was an invasion, so they sent their armies to come protect the king, but later found out that it was just a joke. Seeing all this nonsense happening, Bao Si started laughing. King You was satisfied as he saw Bao Si's smile, and rewarded the sycophant minister with a thousand gold.

一个大臣前来献策说：点燃丽山上的烽火台，取笑一下各路诸侯。那时，烽火台是用来发信号的，当城墙上的士兵看到敌兵进犯周国，便迅速点燃烽火报信。周幽王采纳了这个大臣的建议，命人将烽火台点燃起来。军队的将士以为有敌兵进犯，立即派兵增援救驾。可是，后来发现原来是在开玩笑。看到发生的这一切，褒姒大笑起来。看到褒姒笑了，幽王很高兴，赏赐千金给那个大臣。

Soon after that, there was a real invasion. As the beacon towers were lit up again, the armies took it as another joke and ignored it. The enemy soon took over the State of Zhou, killed King You, and captured Bao Si.

没过多久，烽火台再一次被点燃起来。将士们以为又是在开玩笑，都没
予以理睬。敌军很快攻下周国，周幽王被杀掉，褒姒也被俘虏了。

 Diao Chan
貂蝉

〖Diao Chan〗

Diao Chan is allegedly one of the four ancient Chinese beauties. She was immortalized as a heroine by the well-known Chinese literary classic Romance of Three Kingdoms.　Diao Chan lived before Three Kingdoms Period started.　This was a time when chaos reigned.

One of the warlords, Dong Zhuo, with the help of his god-son Lü Bu, an invincible young warrior, got into power by slaying the child emperor of Han.

貂 蝉

貂 蝉 是 中 国古代四大美女之一 。 在 中 国古典 名著《三国演义》里她作为女英 雄 而 名 垂史书 。 貂 禅 生 于三国时期之前 , 那时天下大乱 , 战 争四起 。

奸雄 董 卓在义子 , 年 轻勇士 , 吕 布 的 帮 助下 , 刺杀了汉 朝 的 年 少皇 帝 , 独揽了朝 政 大权 。

Wang Yun, one of the courtiers that the young emperor had consulted, wanted Dong Zhuo to be killed. However, with Lü Bu as Dong's bodyguard, it was nearly impossible to get near him. Diao Chan was Wang Yun's adopted as a singing-dancing girl. Wang Yun always treated her as his own daughter, for which she was very grateful. Diao Chan decided to help her fatherly master. Together they came up with a plan to destroy Dong Zhuo.

Wang Yun introduced his beautiful Diao Chan to Lü Bu. Lü Bu was immediately captivated by her beauty and was only too happy when Wang Yun offered to marry them in a few days. A day later, Wang Yun played the same trick on Dong Zhuo. Lascivious as

年少皇帝的大臣司徒王允想除掉董卓。然而，有吕布作为董卓的卫士守护在身边，别人几乎无法靠近他。貂禅是王允收下的歌女，王允待她像亲生女儿一样。为此，貂禅心里对王允充满了感激之情。貂禅决心帮助慈爱的主人，他们一起设计要除掉董卓。

王允将美貌的貂禅介绍给吕布。吕布立即为貂禅的美貌所倾倒。当他听说王允答应让他们几日后成婚时，高兴的不得了。过了一天，王允

he was, Dong could not wait and took Diao Chan with him as he left Wang Yun's mansion. Whenever there was a chance, Diao Chan would complain of Lu's harassment before Dong, and her resentment of Dong for nabbing their love before Lu. In so doing, Diao Chan successfully drove a wedge between the father and the son, whose jealousy eventually grew into hatred. One day Dong Zhuo caught Lü Bu courting Diao Chan in his own backyard and became so enraged that he ran after Lü with an attempt to kill him. Father and son became enemies after that. Eventually, Wang Yun successfully convinced Lü Bu to end Dong's life.

又对董卓玩儿起同样的计谋。好色的董卓无法等待，立即把貂禅带出王允的官邸。一有机会，貂禅便向董卓抱怨吕布对她的侵扰，而在吕布面前，貂禅则哭诉董卓对他们爱情的霸占。如此一来，貂禅成功地离间了他们义父子之间的关系，使他们之间由嫉妒而生成怨恨。一天，董卓恰巧撞到吕布和貂禅在后院亲热，他气极败坏追赶吕布，要杀掉他。从此，义父子之间变成仇人。最终，王允说服吕布除掉了董卓。

The Origin of Laba Congee

腊八粥的来历

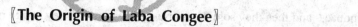

〖The Origin of Laba Congee〗

Once upon a time, a young couple lived with the husband's parents together as a single extended family. The old couple cared for the young couple so much that they did all of the work.   As a result, the young couple never learned how to take care of themselves.

là bā zhōu de lái lì
腊八粥 的来历

hěn jiǔ yǐ qián   yǒu yī jiā rén   ér zǐ   ér xí gēnzhe fù mǔ yī qǐ guò rì zi   lǎo rén duì ér zi
很久以前，有一家人，儿子、儿媳跟着父母一起过日子。 老人对儿子、

ér xí zhào gù de fēi cháng zhōu dào   shén me jiā wù huó er dōu bú ràng tā mendòngshǒu   jié guǒ   xiǎo liǎng kǒu gēn
儿媳照顾得非常 周到，什么家务活儿都不让他们动手 。结果，小俩口根

běn méi yǒu xué huì rú hé zhào gù zì jǐ
本没有学会如何照顾自己 。

Eventually the old couple died. The young couple ate all of the food stored in the house, and then they sold the house to buy food. They had to move into a straw shack. When winter arrived, they were cold and hungry in their shack. On the 8th day of 12th lunar month, they collected a few corn and carrot pieces from the rat hole and made a pot of congee. Just when they were about to eat it, a gust of wind came up and blew down the shed, crushing them to death.

后来，老俩口去世了，小俩口吃完了老人留下的粮食，再后来，他们把房子也卖钱买粮食吃了，最后，他们只好挤在一间破草棚里挨饿。寒冬来了，小俩口又冻又饿，在腊月初八这天，他们从老鼠洞里搜出了一点儿玉米、萝卜，凑合一下，熬成稀粥。正要喝的时候，一阵狂风刮来，把墙刮倒，他们压死在倒塌的墙底下。

Ever since that time, on the 8th day of the 12th lunar month, the festival of Laba, people have made a congee of different grains to remind them of the necessity of knowing how to work.

从此，每到腊月初八，腊八节，这一天人们就用五谷杂粮熬一锅粥，以提醒人们记住劳动生存的道理。

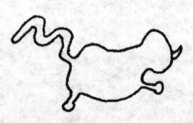

The Earliest Firecrackers

最早的爆竹

〖The Earliest Firecrackers〗

There once were small but terrible monsters called Shansao.   They lived in the forests on the side of mountains in western China.   They were naked and lived on raw shrimp and crabs from the mountain streams.   Sometimes they would steal food from human communities as well.   Fortunately, they were afraid of fires and of loud noises. When people camped out in the mountain, they would light fires and throw in bamboo so that it would make loud bangs as it burned.   This was called "baozhu", "bursting bamboo". Shansao would take fright and flee, leaving people in peace.

最早的爆竹

古时候，有一种 小但可怕的怪物，叫山臊。山臊住在华西的山林里。它们赤身裸体，靠吃山泉里的虾蟹为生。有时，山臊也下山偷食人们的东西。幸亏它们也有所怕，那就是它们害怕火光和噪声。人们在野外露宿时，通常会点上篝火并将竹子投进火中，这样它在燃烧时就会发出噼噼啪啪的声响。人们称之为"爆竹"，意思是"燃烧的竹子"。这时山臊会被吓跑，人们就平安无事了。

In the Tang Dynasty there was a common disease that killed many people. A man named Li Tian put saltpeter inside bamboo tubes and created very loud noise and heavy smoke. People found this an effective way to prevent the disease from spreading. This was the first version of a bamboo tube firecracker.

到了唐朝初期，瘟疫流行，死了很多人。有个叫李田的人，把硝石装在竹筒里，点燃之后就会发出巨大的声响和浓烈的烟雾。人们发现这个办法可以防止疫病扩散流行。这便是竹管爆竹的雏形。

In the Song Dynasty, gunpowder was invented, and it was possible to make paper rolls containing gunpowder that would explode with an even greater sound. These were properly called baozhang, "bursting weapons". Sometimes people put many of them onto a piece of string and light them together, known as "bianpao", or "firecracker". Even today lots of people still say baozhu, in memory of the original exploding bamboo that frightened away the Shansao. And of course, everybody assumes that all sorts of evil forces, and not just Shansao, are frightened by firecrackers.

到了宋朝，又发明了火药。人们把火药装在纸筒里，这样爆炸时就会发出更大的声响。人们给它起名"炮仗"，意思是"燃烧的武器"。有时，人们把很多的炮仗用纸绳系在一起一块儿点燃，人们称之为"编炮"或"鞭炮"。直到今天，仍有很多人叫它"爆竹"，以纪念曾经用来吓唬山臊的"爆炸的竹子"。当然，人们更愿意相信爆竹吓走的不仅有山臊，也包括所有的厄运。

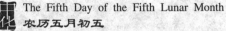

The Fifth Day of the Fifth Lunar Month

农历五月初五

〖The Fifth Day of the Fifth Lunar Month〗

On the fifth day of the fifth lunar month, the day of the Dragon Boat Festival, people eat zongzi. The association of zongzi with this occasion is said to be in memory of the poet Qu Yuan, an official of the State of Chu during the Warring States Period. Qu Yuan was a successful counselor who gave good advice to the King Huai of the Chu State. However, many other officials were jealous of him and persuaded the king to have him banished.

农历五月初五

五月初五是端午节，即龙船节，人们在这一天吃粽子。这种场合吃粽子据说是纪念诗人屈原。屈原是战国时期楚国的大臣，很受楚怀王的重用，曾经向楚怀王提过不少好的政见。可是，很多大臣都妒忌他，怀王听信了他们的谗言，将屈原流放到远方。

In 278 BC, Qin forces, under the command of the famous general Bai Qi, occupied Ying, the Chu capital. Qu Yuan was in despair both at the injustice of his exile and at the loss of his homeland to the Qin conquerors because his advice had not been followed. He commemorated his sorrow in a long poem still widely respected, called "*Leaving the Tumult*". Eventually on the fifth day of the fifth lunar month, overwhelmed by his depression, Qu Yuan committed suicide by jumping into the nearby Miluo River.

gōngyuánqián nián qínjūn zài zhùmíngjiànglǐngbái qǐ de zhǐhuī xià gōng dǎ chǔguó zhànlǐng le chǔguó
公元前 278 年，秦军在著名将领白起的指挥下攻打楚国，占领了楚国

de shǒu dū yǐng qū yuánxiǎng qǐ zì jǐ shòudào bù gōngzhèng de biǎnzhé liúfàngzài wài jiā shanghuáiwáng bù
的首都郢。屈原想起自己受到不公正的贬谪，流放在外，加上怀王不

tīng zì jǐ de jiàn yì shǐ chǔguóbèi qínguómièdiào guórén shī qù le jiā yuán tā bēifèn yù jué tā jiāng zì
听自己的建议；使楚国被秦国灭掉，国人失去了家园，他悲愤欲绝。他将自

jǐ de bēitòngxīnqíngxiě rù yì shǒuchángshī zhōng tí mùjiào lí sāo zhèshǒuchángshī zhì jīn réngshòurén
己的悲痛心情写入一首长诗中，题目叫《离骚》，这首长诗至今仍受人

tuī chóng zuì zhōng zài nóng lì wǔyuèchūwǔ nà yì tiān shī wàngzhì jí de qū yuántóu jìn fù jìn de mì luójiāng
推崇。最终，在农历五月初五那一天，失望至极的屈原投进附近的汨罗江

zì shā
自杀。

People were unable to find Qu Yuan's body. They rowed a boat onto the river, tied the rice into wrappings of bamboo leaves, and throw them into the water to feed the fish and shrimps, so that they wouldn't eat the body of Qu Yuan. Although people do not throw rice into rivers any more, the custom of preparing and eating rice wrapped in bamboo leaves is still associated with the fifth day of the fifth lunar month.

人们无法找到屈原的尸体，便划着船到汨罗江，把用竹叶包好的大米投入江水中喂鱼虾，以免它们会吃了屈原的尸体。后来，尽管人们不再往江里扔米喂鱼虾，但在五月初五那天用竹叶包粽子、吃粽子的习俗却延续了下来。

 A Kid from the Bao Family
鲍家小儿

In the Kingdom of Qi, the Tian family held a ritual to honor their ancestors in the hall. There were more than a thousand guests at the banquet. During the banquet, a guest presented fish and goose dishes.

bào jiā xiǎo ér
鲍家小儿

qí guó de tián shì zài dà tīng lǐ jì sì zǔ xiān qián lái fù yàn de bīn kè duō dá yì qiān duō rén yán xí
齐国的田氏在大厅里祭祀祖先，前来赴宴的宾客多达一千多人。筵席

zhōng yǒu rén xiàn shàng le yú hé é
中，有人献上了鱼和鹅。

Seeing these, Mrs. Tian sighed, "How generous the heavens are to the people! It grows grains and raises fish and birds for people to eat." The guests nodded and echoed with their agreement.

There was a boy from Bao family, only twelve years of age, who also came to the banquet. He stood up and said:

田氏看了，感叹说："上天对待下民太优厚了！它繁殖五谷、生养鱼鸟来供人们食用。"来宾们纷纷点头，随声附和。

鲍家的孩子年仅十二，也来参加宴会。这时他站起来说：

"I'm afraid I can't agree with you. All the different categories of natural beings just happen to live on the earth with us. There isn't any high or low status levels among all these creatures. The food link is based on the size and intelligence, but no creature was created for another. People eat what they can get, but it doesn't mean things were specially created for people to eat. In fact, mosquitoes bite us, the tigers and wolves eat us, but can we follow this logic and say people were created for mosquitoes, tigers and wolves?"

"我不能同意您的说法。天地万物与我们共同生存，类与类之间没有高贵和低贱之分，食物链只是凭个头的大小以及智慧的分别而相互制约，迭次相食，不存在谁为谁生的道理。人们拿可以吃的东西来吃，但这并不意味这些东西是上天特意为了人类而创造的。事实上，蚊虫叮人，虎狼吃人，可是我们能照上面的逻辑说是上天为了它们而特地创造了人类吗？"

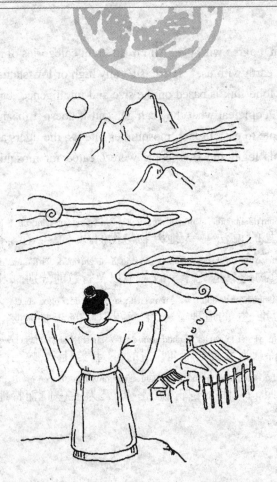

A Haven of Peace and Happiness
世外桃源

中国传统文化经典故事100篇·英汉对照

236

〖A Haven of Peace and Happiness〗

Tao Yuanming, a famous writer of the Eastern Jin Dynasty, wrote the well-known essay *Peach-Blossom Spring*. In it he tells a story which goes like this: A fisherman happened to come upon a place called Peach-Blossom Spring. Squeezing through a cave, he found a village, the residents of which were descendants of refugees from the Qin Dynasty. It was a paradise isolated from the outside world, without exploitation or oppression, and everybody living and working in peace and contentment. The fisherman left the villagers and went home. But he could never find the place again.

This idiom is derived from the above story, and is used to mean an isolated, ideal world.

世外桃源

东晋的著名文学家陶渊明写了一篇著名的文章叫《桃花源记》。文章讲述了一个故事：一个渔人出外捕鱼的时候，偶然来到了桃花源这个地方。通过一个山洞，他发现了一个村子，村里的居民是秦朝时避难人的后代。这是一个与世隔绝、没有剥削和压迫、人人安居乐业的美好的乐园。渔人告别村民回家以后，再也找不到这个地方了。

后来，由这个故事产生了"世外桃源"这个成语，用来比喻与世隔绝的、理想的美好社会。

中国传统文化经典故事100篇·英汉对照

 Xiyong and the Bandits
郗雍与盗贼

〖Xiyong and the Bandits〗

Once upon a time, the Kingdom of Jin had many bandits. There was a man named Xiyong, who could judge if a person was a bandit by observing his appearance. Xiyong went on missions of catching bandits, and he finished more than one thousand and had never failed one of them.

xì yōng yǔ dào zéi
郤 雍 与 盗贼

cóngqián jìn guó de dào zéi hěn duō yǒu yí gè jiào xì yōng de rén zhǐ yào tōngguòguānchá qí xiàngmào
从 前 ，晋国的盗贼很多 。 有一个叫郤雍的人，只要通过观察其相貌，

jiù néngjiànbié yí gè rén shì fǒu shì dào zéi tā fèngmìng qù zhuō zéi qiānbǎi gè dāngzhōng bù céng yí lòu yí
就 能 鉴别一个人是否是盗贼 。 他奉命去捉贼，千百个当中不曾遗漏一

gè
个 。

Soon, the bandits gathered together and discussed, "It is Xiyong who has caused our current desperate situation." They took action and killed Xiyong.

The king was shocked by the death of Xiyong and he immediately summoned Wenzi, the intelligent minister, and asked him, "Xiyong was killed! How in the world can we catch those bandits now?"

guò le bù jiǔ　　dào zéi men jù jí zài yī qǐ　　hù xiāng shāng liang shuō　　wǒ men zhī suǒ yǐ zǒu tóu wú
过了不久，盗贼们聚集在一起，互相商量说："我们之所以走投无

lù　wán quán shì xì yōng zào chéng de　　　yú shì　jiù xíng dòng qǐ lái　shā sǐ le xì yōng
路，完全是郄雍造成的。"于是，就行动起来，杀死了郄雍。

jìn guó guó jūn tīng shuō xì yōng bèi shā　dà wéi jīng hài　lì jí zhào jiàn móu shì wén zǐ bìng duì tā shuō　　xì
晋国国君听说郄雍被杀，大为惊骇，立即召见谋士文子并对他说："郄

yōng bèi shā sǐ le　xiàn zài wǒ men yòng shén me fāng fǎ lái zhuō ná dào zéi ne
雍被杀死了！现在我们用什么方法来捉拿盗贼呢？"

中国传统文化经典故事100篇·英汉对照

Wenzi said, "If you really want to destroy them, just appoint intelligent people in your government to carry out the policies and to improve the education. Nobody will want to be a bandit when he knows what is right and wrong."

The king took Wenzi's advice, and soon after that, the bandits all ran to another kingdom.

文子说："国君想要真正消灭盗贼，不如招揽并任用贤才，使政令严明于上，教化风行于下，这样就没人去做强盗了。"

于是，晋国国君采纳了文子的意见。不久，盗贼们纷纷逃到别的国去了。

名聲

Describing Reputation

关于名声

〖Describing Reputation〗

When Yangzhu was traveling around the Kingdom of Lu, he stayed with his friend Meng. One day, Meng asked him, "Why do people always pursue reputation even though they already are wealthy with a high social status?"

Yangzhu said, "For their offspring."

Meng asked: "What can one's good reputation do for his offspring?"

guān yú míngshēng
关于名声

yáng zhū zài lǔ guó yóu lì　zhù zài hào péng yǒu mèng shì jiā lǐ　yí cì　mèng shì wèn tā　rén men yǒu le
杨朱在鲁国游历，住在好朋友孟氏家里。一次，孟氏问他："人们有了

cái fù hé zūn guì de dì wèi　wèi shén me hái yào hǎo míng shēng ne
财富和尊贵的地位，为什么还要好名声呢？"

yáng zhū dá　wèi le tā men de zǐ sūn hòu dài
杨朱答："为了他们的子孙后代。"

mèng shì wèn　hǎo míng shēng duì yú zǐ sūn yǒu shén me hǎo chù ne
孟氏问："好名声对于子孙有什么好处呢？"

Yangzhu replied, "Someone who has a good reputation can make his wealth and credibility last. His offspring, and even other people from his descent, from his city, can all benefit from their predecessors!"

Meng said, "People who pursue a good reputation must be honest and modest, which makes them poor and humble."

Yangzhu said, "When Guanzhong was the Prime Minister of King Qihuangong, the king passed his days with luxurious ease and Guanzhong did the same thing. To have the same interest with the king, Guanzhong made all his policies carried out easily all over

yángzhū dá
杨朱答："有好名声的人能把他的财富和信誉延续下去。 他的子孙后

dài nǎi zhì tā de tóng zú tóngxiāng dōu kě yǐ cóngxiānrén de míngshēngzhōngshòu yì
代，乃至他的同族、同乡都可以从先人的名声中受益。"

mèngshì shuō fán shì zhuī qiúmíngshēng de rén bì ránzhèngzhí qiānràng ér zhèngzhí qiānràng fǎn ér huì
孟氏说："凡是追求名声的人必然正直谦让，而正直谦让反而会

shǐ tā pínkùn bēi wēi
使他贫困、卑微。"

yángzhū shuō guǎnzhòngzuòwéiguóxiàng fǔ zuǒ qí huánggōng de shíhou guójūnguòzheqīngsōng zì rú de
杨朱说："管仲作为国相辅佐齐桓公的时候，国君过着轻松自如的

shēnghuó tā yě hé guójūn yí yàngguò de cóngróng zì rú cóng ér shǐ tā de zhìguózhí dào dé yǐ shùn lì tuī
生活，他也和国君一样过得从容自如，从而使他的治国之道得以顺利推

the kingdom, which made this kingdom the most powerful kingdom among all the king-doms. However, since Guanzhong didn't pursue the reputation, his family declined after his death. Another Prime Minister Tian chengzi was just the reverse. After Tian Chengzi was inaugurated as the Prime Minister, he was very modest when the king was in lordly manners, and he supported the poor people when the king gathered the wealth from his territory. This Prime Minister easily took over the power of the kingdom after he won the people. Today, his offspring are still enjoying the benefit he brought them. True people don't care about reputation, while people who have a good reputation aren't necessarily sincere. The difference between true and false is so clear!"

行，齐国得以称霸天下。然而，由于管仲并不求名声，他的家族在他死后就败落下来。另一位国相田成子却正相反。他出任齐国相国后，国君骄盈，他却谦逊；国君聚敛财货，他却施舍济贫。取得了民心之后，便轻易地掌握了齐国的大权。直到今天，他的子孙仍享用他的福泽。真实的人不在乎名声，有好名声的人不必真实。真实和虚假的分别，就是这样地清楚啊！"

中国传统文化经典故事100篇·英汉对照

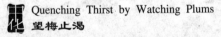

Quenching Thirst by Watching Plums
望梅止渴

〖Quenching Thirst by Watching Plums〗

One summer, Cao Cao was leading his troops in a punitive expedition against Zhang Xiu. It was extraordinarily hot. The burning sun was like a fire, and the sky was cloudless. The soldiers were walking on the winding mountain paths. The dense forest and the hot rocks exposed to the sun on both sides of the paths made the soldiers feel suffocated. By noontime the soldiers' clothes were wet with sweat, and the marching speed slowed down. Some soldiers of weak physique even fainted on the roadside.

wàngméizhǐ kě

望 梅 止 渴

yǒu yì nián xià tiān cáocāoshuàilǐng bù duì qù tǎo fá zhāngxiù tiān qì rè de chū qí jiāoyáng sì huǒ
有一年夏天，曹操 率 领部队去讨伐 张 绣，天气热得出奇，骄阳似火，

tiānshàng yī sī yúncai yě méiyǒu bù duì zài wānwān qū qū de shān lù shàngxíngzǒu liǎngbiān mì mì de shùmù hé
天 上 一丝云彩也没有，部队在弯 弯曲曲的山路 上 行走，两 边密密的树木和

bèi yángguāngshài de gǔntàng de shān shí ràngrén tòu bú guò qì lái dào le zhōngwǔ shí fēn shì bīng de yī fu dōu
被阳 光 晒得滚烫的山石，让人透不过气来。到了 中 午时分，士兵的衣服都

shī tòu le xíngjūn de sù dù yě mànxià lái yǒu jǐ gè tǐ ruò de shì bīngjìngyūndǎozài lù biān
湿透了，行军的速度也慢下来，有几个体弱的士兵竟晕倒在路边 。

Seeing that the marching speed was slower and slower, Cao Cao was very worried because he feared that he might bungle the chance of winning the battle. But how could they quicken their speed in that situation? Cao Cao at once called the guide and asked him on the quiet whether there was a source of water nearby. The guide shook his head, saying that the spring water was on the other side of the mountain, which was very far to reach. Cao Cao realized that time didn't permit them to make such a detour. After looking at the front forest and thinking for a moment, he said to the guide, "Keep quiet. I'll find a way out." He knew that it would be to no avail to order his troops to quicken the steps. He had a brain wave and found a good solution. He spurred his horse and came to

曹操看行军的速度越来越慢，担心贻误战机，心里很是着急。可是，眼下情形，又怎么能加快速度呢？他立刻叫来向导，悄悄问他："这附近可有水源？"向导摇摇头说："泉水在山谷的那一边，要绕道过去还有很远的路程。"曹操想了一下说，"不行，时间来不及。"他看了看前边的树林，沉思了一会儿，对向导说："你什么也别说，我来想办法。"他知道此刻即使下命令要求部队加快速度也无济于事。脑筋一转，办法来了，他

the head of the column. Pointing his horsewhip to the front, Cao Cao said, "Soldiers, I know there is a big forest of plums ahead. The plums there are both big and delicious. Let's hurry along, and we will reach the forest of plums after bypassing this hill." When the soldiers heard this, they immediately slobbered. The soldiers felt as if they were actually eating the plums. The morale greatly boosted, the soldiers quickened their steps a great deal automatically.

一夹马肚子，快速赶到队伍前面，用马鞭指着前方说："士兵们，我知道前面有一大片梅林，那里的梅子又大又好吃，我们快点儿赶路，绕过这个山丘就到梅林了！"士兵们一听，仿佛已经吃到嘴里，精神大振，步伐不由得加快了许多。

The Tale of Nian
关于"年"的传说

〖The Tale of Nian〗

Long ago there lived a frightful demon called Nian (year), with a single large horn, heavy green scales, a huge mouth, and very sharp teeth. And, being a frightful demon, of course it did evil things wherever it went. Because it was so dangerous, the demon was locked by the heavenly gods into a remote mountain prison —some people say in the sea. It was permitted to leave only once every twelve months so that it would not starve.

guān yú nián de chuánshuō
关于"年"的传说

cóngqián yǒu yí gè guàishòu míng zi jiào nián nián tóuzhǎng dújiǎo shēnzhǎng lù lín
从前,有一个怪兽,名字叫"年"。"年"头长独角,身长绿鳞,

zuǐ bā shuò dà yá chǐ fēng lì xiōngměng yì cháng hěn zì rán xiōngměng de nián wú lùn zǒu dào nǎ
嘴巴硕大,牙齿锋利,凶猛异常。很自然,凶猛的"年"无论走到哪

er dōu huì dài lái zāi nàn yīn wéi tā yǒu rú cǐ wēi hài suǒ yǐ tiānshén bǎ tā qiú jìn zài yuǎnshānzhī zhōng yǒu
儿,都会带来灾难。因为它有如此危害,所以天神把它囚禁在远山之中,有

rén shuō shì qiú jìn zài hǎi lǐ wèi le bú ràng nián è sǐ tiānshényǔn xǔ tā měi shí èr gè yuèchū lái yí
人说是囚禁在海里。为了不让"年"饿死,天神允许它每十二个月出来一

cì
次。

Unfortunately Nián's yearly release was very difficult for humans, for every year it would come down from its prison to the villages very hungry indeed and would look for food and for villagers to eat. Frightened villagers would put out some of their livestock in hope of satisfying its appetite while they themselves hid inside their houses or fled into the mountains to hide.

不幸的是每年释放"年"这怪兽,可害苦了百姓,因为它从囚禁地来到村庄时,已经饿得要命,见到粮食就吃,见到村民也不放过。吓坏了的村民往往拿出他们的家畜给它吃,希望能满足它的食欲,而他们自己却躲在屋子里或逃到山上藏起来。

But one year an odd old beggar happened to be visiting the village on the day when the Nián monster was due to be released. Everyone fled in a panic, leaving the old beggar in the village to be devoured by the monster. The old beggar took refuge inside a house. There happened to be a piece of red paper fluttering from the door of a house, and it attracted the attention of the Nian monster, but as it charged the door, it happened to be hit by lightning, which hurt quite a bit, so that his scream was almost as loud as the peal of thunder. Slowly recovering, the monster more cautiously circulated through the village, avoiding anything red, for it was now afraid.

有一年，一个年老的乞丐恰巧在白天怪兽要来的时候来到村里。人们都惊慌失措藏起来，剩下年老的乞丐将要被怪兽吃掉。老人躲进一所房子里。恰巧房门里飘出一张红纸条。这张红纸条吸引了"年"的注意力，可是当它冲向门口时，却碰巧被闪电击中，伤得不轻。"年"的尖叫声像轰鸣的雷声。慢慢地"年"醒过神来后，它害怕任何红色的东西，在村子里行走更加谨慎了。

When the Nian monster showed fear, the old beggar got an idea. He found some red cloth and wound himself up in it, then emerged into the lane, lighting and throwing the largest firecrackers he could find. The monster saw a red figure coming toward him carrying a bright lantern and making sounds like thunder, and turned and fled in terror. Once they discovered that the Nian monster was afraid of red color, and bright lanterns, and loud, thunderous noises, the villagers knew how to protect themselves. So each year, when he was released, people would light up their houses, and would paster paper on their doors and wear red clothes, and would set off firecrackers and beat gongs and drums.

看到年的恐惧，老乞丐有了主意。他找了一块儿红布把自己裹起来，然后出现在巷子里，他找到最大的爆竹，一边点燃，一边投掷。怪兽看到一个红色的人影提着灯笼，发出雷鸣般的响声，朝他走来，吓得他立即逃走了。村民们一经发现怪兽害怕红色、灯笼和响声，便明白应该如何保护自己了。于是，每年怪兽出来时，人们就会点亮灯火，房门贴上红纸，身穿红色的衣服，并且燃放鞭炮、敲锣打鼓。

中国传统文化经典故事100篇·英汉对照

No one got much sleep on that day, but the cowardly monster never troubled them again. And so on the morning of each New Year, they could rejoice and congratulate each other on avoiding disaster, and wish each other great happiness for the year that was so well begun.

这一天，没人睡多少觉，不过胆怯的怪兽再也没来骚扰他们了。从此，每当新年来临，人们就会欢天喜地相互道贺，祝福新年大吉，无灾无难，幸福快乐。

Power of Skirts
裙子的力量

【Power of Skirts】

In a field in the Liangshan Mountain, two groups of young men from the Chinese Yi nationality armed with spears, sticks and bows are on the verge of a violent fight. Suddenly, a middle-aged woman dressed in a skirt edged with lace comes between them. The sharp spears almost touch her body, but she remains calm and shakes her skirt as if she is signaling the men. The fighters are all astonished by the sudden scene. They stop forwarding and slowly lower their arms, watching the waving of the skirt. After a moment's silence, the heads of both sides order to withdraw.

qún zǐ de lì liang

裙子的力量

在凉山山区，彝族的两个部落的年轻人正挎着弓箭、持棒荷戟，一场械斗一触即发。突然，只见一个中年妇女她穿着一条镶嵌着花边的裙子站在对峙的两群人之间。尖锐的利器几乎触及到她的身体，而她却保持着十分的平静，舞动着长裙，仿佛在发出什么信号。斗士们对着突发的场面惊呆了。他们停止进攻，慢慢放下武器，观看着她的长裙漫舞。沉默片刻后，双方的头儿便各自下了撤退令。

Who is that woman? Is she a powerful authority from a village? No! She is only an ordinary woman. The fact is that one group of the young men are from her husband's village and the other from her own. According to the customs of Yi in that area, if an armed fight ever happens between two villages, no man from either village dare go to the border by risking being kidnapped or killed. Women, however, are exceptional. As usual, they can work in fields along the border or visit relatives and friends in the opposite village without being endangered. If another war should happen, any woman from the related village mediate in it by standing between the fighting parties. Her action is usually respected. If either of the two sides ignores her advice, she will put off her skirt and stand naked before them until she commits suicide for the sake of honor. If such an event does

那个妇女是谁？她是村里的权威人士吗？不，她只是一个普通的妇女。实际上对峙的双方一方来自她婆家的村落，一方来自她娘家的村落。根据彝族的风俗，如果双方发生械斗，就没有人敢冒着被绑架或被杀死的危险再踏入另一个村落。然而女人却可以例外。她们可以像往常一样沿着村界在田里干活或者访亲会友而不会有什么危险。如果另一场械斗即将发生，任何一方的妇女都可以站在对峙双方的中间。她的行为通常会受到尊重。如果双方不理睬她，她就会脱下裙子赤身站在那里，直到为了名誉而

happen, the side who sticks to the war will be condemned and more people will join the war. As large scale wars are discouraged, the brave woman's advice is often favored by the fighters.

自杀。如果这类事情发生的话，坚持打仗的一方就会受到谴责，而且会有更多的人加入战斗。大规模的战争是招人反对的，勇敢女士的忠告通常受到斗士们的首肯。

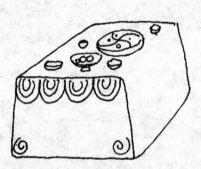

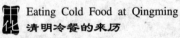

Eating Cold Food at Qingming

清明冷餐的来历

〖Eating Cold Food at Qingming〗

During the Spring and Autumn Period, Chong Er, the son of a duke of the State of Jin, was forced to live in exile for 19 years. When he eventually succeeded his father as duke and was able to return to Jin, he granted titles and land to his followers. However, he neglected to provide anything for Jie Zhitui, one of his most devoted supporters. Jie Zhitui was devastated at this ingratitude, and, bearing his mother on his back, he went into the forests in Mian Mountain to live.

清明冷餐的来历

春秋时期，晋国公的儿子重耳被流放了十九年。后来他终于回到晋国，继承王位。于是他赏赐给许多追随他的门客以官职和土地，却冷落了一个对他最忠心的，名叫介之推的门客。介之推心灰意冷，将他的母亲背在背上，走到绵山的森林里去隐居。

When Chong Er heard about this, he sent men to seek out Jie, but the mountain forest was too large, and they were unable to find him. Chong Er ordered to set fire to the forest, hoping to drive Jie and his mother out on the other side. As the fire moved through the trees, nobody came out.

重耳听说此事，派人去寻找介之推。可是深山老林面积太大了，重耳的人无法找到他。于是重耳命人放火点燃森林，希望能借助火势的推进，将介之推从森林的另一边逼出来。可是，大火烧遍了整个森林，还是没有人出来。

Jie Zhitui and his mother were later found burned to death in the forest. Chong Er was deeply saddened. In commemoration, he ordered that all the fires of the land of Jin be extinguished, and that only cold food be eaten on that day.

And that is the origin of the Cold Food Feast associated with Qingming, the festival of the ancestors.

后来，介之推母子的尸体被发现了，是被大火烧死的。 重耳为此事深深的悲痛。 为了纪念介之推， 重耳下令，在这一天，全国都不准使用火，大家只吃冷餐。

这就是清明节吃冷餐的来历。

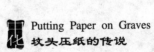

Putting Paper on Graves

坟头压纸的传说

〖Putting Paper on Graves〗

Liu Bang was the triumphant general who ended years of chaos and successfully established the Han Dynasty, and history knows him as its first emperor under the title "great ancestor".

After his great success, he returned to celebrate at his native village. However, his parents were no longer alive to enjoy his success, and indeed in the chaos of the war, nobody remembered any longer which graves were theirs.

坟头压纸的传说

刘邦是汉朝的第一个皇帝,他成功地结束了多年的战乱,建立了汉朝,历史上称之为"汉高祖"。

登基后,刘邦回到故乡举办庆典,却发现他的父母已经过世了。当地连年战乱,已经没人知道二老的坟在什么地方。

As the new emperor and his minions were seeking in despair through the cemetery of the village, he noticed some pieces of colored paper floating in the breeze, a local custom for communicating with supernaturals. In a moment of inspiration, he gathered a handful of these papers and threw them into the air, praying that they would reveal the location of his parents' tomb. Suddenly, they all floated at once to a single grave.

liú bāng dài zhe shǒu xià rén jué wàng de zài fén dì lǐ xún zhǎo fā xiàn yì xiē cǎi sè de zhǐ piàn zài kōng zhōng fēi

刘邦带着手下人绝望地在坟地里寻找，发现一些彩色的纸片在空中飞

yáng yuán lái zhè shì dāng dì de fēng sú yòng zhǐ piàn lái jì bài shén líng liú bāng líng jī yí dòng zhuā

扬。 原来这是当地的风俗，用纸片来祭拜神灵。 刘邦灵机一动，抓

le yī bǎ zhǐ piàn yíng fēng rēng le chū qù xīn zhōng mò mò dǎo zhù zhè xiē zhǐ piàn zhǐ yǐn zhèng què de fāng xiàng

了一把纸片，迎风扔了出去，心中默默祷祝这些纸片指引正确的方向，

zhǐ jiàn zhè xiē zhǐ piàn fēi dào le yí gè fén shàng luò le xià lái

只见这些纸片飞到了一个坟上落了下来。

The emperor declared this to be the correct grave, and ordered a large monument erected. Ever since that time when people have cleaned their ancestors' graves at Qingming, they put bits of paper on top, weighted down by stones, to show that the descendants are filially paying attention to the remains of their ancestors.

liú bāng xuān bù　zhè jiù shì èr lǎo de fén　bìng zài cǐ jiàn le yí zuò jù dà de mù bēi　cóng nà shí qǐ
刘邦宣布，这就是二老的坟，并在此建了一座巨大的墓碑。从那时起，

měi nián qīng míng jié rén men sǎo mù de shí hòu　dōu yào zài mù bēi shang yòng shí tou yā jǐ piàn zhǐ　lái biǎo shì hòu dài
每年清明节人们扫墓的时候，都要在墓碑上用石头压几片纸，来表示后代

duì zǔ xiān yí tǐ de zūn zhòng
对祖先遗体的尊重。

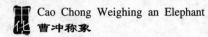 Cao Chong Weighing an Elephant
曹冲称象

268

〖Cao Chong Weighing an Elephant〗

Once upon a time during the Period of the Three Kingdoms in China, King Sun of Wu gave an elephant to King Cao of Wei as a present. So King Cao and his men all went to see the elephant. His young son Prince Chong also came along. At that time Prince Chong was only a little child.

"Who would know how to figure out the weight of this awesome creature?" King Cao asked. One official suggested building a jumbo weighing device. A general thought it would be simple to cut the elephant to pieces, weigh the pieces and then add up the total.

cáochōng chēng xiàng
曹冲称象

zài sānguóshí qī wú wáng sūnquánsòng le yì zhī dà xiàng gěi wèi wáng cáocāo zuò lǐ wù cáocāo jí shǒuxià
在三国时期，吴王孙权送了一只大象给魏王曹操作礼物。曹操及手下

de guānyuánmendōu qù kàn dà xiàng bāokuò tā de ér zi cáochōng cáochōng dāng shí hái zhǐ shì ge xiǎohái zi
的官员们都去看大象，包括他的儿子曹冲。曹冲当时还只是个小孩子。

shuínéngxiǎngbàn fǎ chēngchūzhè ge dà jiā huo de zhòngliang cáocāowèndào yí gè wénguānjiàn
"谁能想办法称出这个大家伙的重量？"曹操问道。一个文官建

yì zào yì gǎn dà chèng bǎ xiàngfàngshàng qù chēng yí gè wǔjiàngquè tí chūgāncuì bǎ xiàngqiē chéng yí kuài
议造一杆大秤，把象放上去称。一个武将却提出干脆把象切成一块

ér kuài ér de fēn biéchēng zài bǎ zhòngliangjiā qǐ lái
儿块儿的分别称，再把重量加起来。

All the king's men were coming up with ideas but none of them were feasible.　At this time Prince Chong walked up to his father and said,　"I have a way to find out how much the elephant weighs."

Prince Chong whispered in the King's ear and made him smile.　The King relented and said to his men, "This little boy of mine seems to have a good idea. Let's all go and see how he does it."

dà jiā qī zuǐ bā shé　quèméiyǒu yí gè rénxiǎng de chū yí gè kě xíng de hǎobàn fǎ　zhèng zài zhè gè shí
大家七嘴八舌，却没有一个人想得出一个可行的好办法。正在这个时

hou cáochōngpǎochū lái zhàndào dà renmiànqiánshuō　wǒyǒubàn fǎ chēngchū dà xiàng de zhòngliang
候，曹冲跑出来站到大人面前说："我有办法称出大象的重量！"

cáochōngzài tā fù qīncáocāo de ěr biānshuō le jǐ jù huà　cáocāotīng le　xiàozhedùiguānyuánmenshuō
曹冲在他父亲曹操的耳边说了几句话。曹操听了，笑着对官员们说：

zhèháizi sì hū yǒu yí gè zhǔ yì　zánmen qù kànkan tā shì zěnme chēng dà xiàng de
"这孩子似乎有一个主意，咱们去看看他是怎么称大象的。"

Prince Chong had the elephant led to the river. The whole crowd followed behind. There was a big boat along the river. Prince Chong told the handler to bring the elephant on board and mark the water level on the side of the boat. He then had the elephant led onshore again. After that, Prince Chong asked the aides to bring loads of rocks and put them on the boat until the boat reached the same water level as marked. Then they simply had to weigh the rocks and add up the total. By now, all the adults realized how clever a way it was to solve the problem.

曹冲叫人牵了大象，跟着他到河边去。曹操和官员们一起跟着来到河边。河边正好有只大船，曹冲让人把大象牵到船上，大象上了船，船就往下沉了一些。曹冲说："齐水面在船帮上划一道记号。"记号划好了以后，曹冲又叫人把大象牵上岸来。接下来曹冲叫人挑了石块，一块儿一块儿地装到大船上去，大船又慢慢地往下沉了，直到船帮上的记号齐了水面，再把石块一块儿一块儿在秤上称，然后把份量加在一起便得出大象的重量。这时候，大人们才明白这是一个多么聪明的解决问题的方法啊。

 Bole and Thousand–mile Horse
伯乐与千里马

〖Bole and Thousand-mile Horse〗

The king of Kingdom Qin loved good horses.　Once he said to Bole,　the famous horse seeker,　"You are getting old.　Do you have anybody to recommend among your sons and grandsons who can be a good horse seeker?" Bole replied, "A good horse can be recognized by its body shape,　appearance,　muscles and its frame,　but this doesn't work for the best horse, the very rare 'thousand-mile'. A 'thousand-mile' looks very indistinct and capricious.　However once it starts to run,　all its hooves seem to be running over the ground without touching the dust, and the wheels of the cart wheel as fast as the wind, without leaving a track on the ground.　Jiu Fanggao is my friend who gathered firewood

bó lè yǔ qiān lǐ mǎ

伯乐与千里马

秦国国君秦穆公最爱好马。　一次他对善于相马的伯乐说："您已经老了，您的子孙当中有没有善于寻找良马的人呢？"伯乐回答说："一匹好马可以通过它的形体、外貌、筋肉和骨骼来鉴别。至于天下罕有的千里马则不然，它们看上去迷离恍惚，很难捉摸。这样的马一旦奔跑起来，蹄子就好像离开地面，不沾尘土；马车的轮子运转如风，不在地上留下辙印。我有一位与我一同打柴的朋友，名叫九方皋，他相马的本领不在我之下。

273

with me. He is as good as me in seeking horses. Please allow me to recommend him to you."

The king summoned Jiu Fanggao and sent him to find a "thousand-mile". Three months later, Jiu Fanggao came back and reported to the king, "I've found it, right in Shaqiu." The king asked, "What's it like?" Jiu Fanggao said, "It's a yellow mare." The king sent people to get the yellow mare, but found it a black colt. The king was unhappy. He summoned Bole and said to him, "The man you recommended to seek the 'thousand-mile' is horrible! He couldn't even tell the color and gender of a horse! How can he tell the quality of a horse?"

qǐng yǔn xǔ wǒ dài tā lái jiàn nín
请允许我带他来见您。"

qín mù gōng zhào jiàn le jiǔ fāng gāo   pài tā qù xún zhǎo qiān lǐ mǎ   sān gè yuè zhī hòu   jiǔ fāng gāo huí lái
秦穆公召见了九方皋，派他去寻找千里马。三个月之后，九方皋回来

bào gào   zhǎo dào le   jiù zài shā qiū   qín mù gōng wèn   nà shì zěn yàng de yì pǐ mǎ ne   jiǔ
报告："找到了，就在沙丘。"秦穆公问："那是怎样的一匹马呢？"九

fāng gāo huí dá   shì yì pǐ huáng sè de cí mǎ   qín mù gōng pài rén qù qǔ nà pǐ huáng sè de cí mǎ   què
方皋回答："是一匹黄色的雌马。"秦穆公派人去取那匹黄色的雌马，却

fā xiàn qǔ huí lái de shì yì pǐ hēi sè de xióng mǎ   qín mù gōng bù gāo xìng le   zhào jiàn bó lè bìng duì tā shuō
发现取回来的是一匹黑色的雄马。秦穆公不高兴了，召见伯乐并对他说：

nǐ tuī jiàn de nà ge zhǎo mǎ rén zhēn zāo gāo a   lián mǎ de máo sè   cí xióng dōu fēn biàn bù qīng   yòu rú hé
"你推荐的那个找马人真糟糕啊！连马的毛色、雌雄都分辨不清，又如何

néng shí bié mǎ de yōu liè ne
能识别马的优劣呢？"

Bole gave out a deep sigh and said, "He has reached this level! This is why he is a much better horse seeker than me! What Jiu Fanggao sees in a horse is its talent. He observes the vital element of a horse but ignores the other. He sees the essential characteristics but ignores the appearance. He only sees what he needs to see and to pay attention to what he should attach importance to.

The horse arrived, and it was indeed a very rare "thousand-mile" horse.

伯乐听了，长叹一声道："他竟然到了这种境界！这正是他比我高明千万倍的地方啊！九方皋所看到的，是马的天赋，他观察到马的本质因素而忽略其次要因素，发现马的内在特质而忽略马的外观形象。他只看他需要看的东西，注意他认为重要的东西。"

马被取回来了，果然是一匹天下稀有的千里马。

 A Reunited Mirror
破镜重圆

〖 A Reunited Mirror 〗

In the Northern and Southern Dynasties, Chen Shubao, the last king of the State of Chen, had a sister named Princess Le Chang, who married a man named Xu Deyan.

pò jìng chóng yuán
破镜重圆

nán běi cháo shí qī　　chén cháo zuì hòu yí gè huáng dì chén shū bǎo yǒu yí gè mèi mei　　rén men jiào tā lè chāng
南北朝时期，陈朝最后一个皇帝陈叔宝有一个妹妹，人们叫她乐昌

gōng zhǔ　　lè chāng gōng zhǔ jià gěi le xú dé yán wéi qī
公主，乐昌公主嫁给了徐德言为妻。

Seeing that Chen was facing its demise, Xu Deyan said to his wife, "Once the state falls, you will be taken by some powerful men because you have good looks. If we are meant to be together we shall reunite eventually, and here is what we use to meet again." Xu broke a bronze mirror into halves. Each of them kept a half as tokens in case they were separated. Xu said, "Every year on the 15th of first lunar month, go to sell your half of mirror on the market. If I'm still alive, I'll find you."

眼见陈朝日益衰微，徐德言对妻子说："国家一旦灭亡，你就会因容貌姣好而被强敌掠走，如果我们要团聚，最终会团聚的，这就是我们再见面时的信物。"徐德言将一面铜镜破为两半，自己留一半，另一半给妻子，接着说："每年正月十五那天，你在集市上卖这半面镜子，如果我还活着，我会去找你。"

Soon afterwards, the State of Chen was overthrown. Princess Le Chang was taken into the home of Sui minister Yang Su. Overcoming many obstacles, Xu was finally able to get back to the capital city. On the 15th of first lunar month, Xu came to the market and saw a man selling the half mirror with high price. Xu took the man to his place, put the two perfectly fitting halves of mirror together, and told the man to take it to the princess. Hearing this story, Yang Su let the princess go back to Xu. The couple lived happily ever after.

陈朝亡国后，乐昌公主果然落入了隋朝大臣杨素家里。徐德言历经千难万险、流离颠沛，终于回到了京城。正月十五这天，他来到集市上，看到有人正在高价叫卖半面镜子，徐德言将那人领到住处，那人所卖的半面镜子与自己的半面镜子正好合在了一起，托卖镜之人带给公主。杨素知道了这件事，放手让公主和徐德言团聚，二人终于白头偕老。

Three Movings by Mencius' Mother
孟母三迁之教

〖Three Movings by Mencius' Mother〗

Mencius, one of the greatest thinkers in Chinese history, was born in the Warring States Period. After his father's death when he was three, Mencius was raised by his mother. Mencius' mother was an educated woman and took her son's education very seriously.

When young, Mencius enjoyed playing with other kids. Their original house was located near a large area of tombs. He, with other pals, would play the game of digging and mounding graves.

mèng mǔ sān qiān zhī jiào
孟母三迁之教

mèng zǐ míng kē   shì wǒ guó lì shǐ shàng zhùmíng de sī xiǎng jiā   shēng yú zhàn guó shí qī   tā sān suì sàng
孟子名珂,是我国历史上著名的思想家,生于战国时期。他三岁丧

fù   yóu mǔ qīn fǔ yǎng zhǎng dà   mèng mǔ shì ge hěn yǒu jiào yǎng de fù nǚ   fēi cháng zhòng shì duì ér zi de jiào
父,由母亲抚养长大。孟母是个很有教养的妇女,非常重视对儿子的教

yù
育。

mèng zǐ xiǎo shí hou jīng cháng hé huǒ bàn men yì qǐ wán er   mèng jiā fù jìn yǒu yí kuài mù dì   yú shì
孟子小时候经常和伙伴们一起玩儿。孟家附近有一块墓地,于是,

mèng zǐ hé xiǎo huǒ bàn men yì qǐ wán er wā kēng zhù fén de yóu xì
孟子和小伙伴们一起玩儿挖坑筑坟的游戏。

Mencius' mother was angry and thought this environment wasn't good for her son's growth. She decided to move their home into the city.

However, they now lived in the middle of a loud market, and Mencius couldn't sit down to read. He and his friends started playing trading games. Again, Mencius' mother thought it was not a good environment for a child to concentrate on studies. They moved to the east of city.

mèng mǔ duì ér zi zhè yàng wán shuǎ hěn shēng qì rèn wéi zhè zhǒng huán jìng bú lì yú tā chéng zhǎng biàn bǎ
孟母对儿子这样玩耍很生气，认为这种环境不利于他成长，便把

jiā qiān dào le chéng lǐ
家迁到了城里。

kě shì yóu yú xīn jiā chǔ yú nào shì mèng zǐ hái shì wú fǎ qián xīn dú shū tā yòu hé xiǎo huǒ bàn men wán qǐ
可是由于新家处于闹市，孟子还是无法潜心读书。他又和小伙伴们玩起

le zuò mǎi mai de yóu xì mèng mǔ jué de zài zhè gè dì fang jū zhù yě hěn nán jí zhōng xīn sī dú shū biàn zài cì bān
了做买卖的游戏，孟母觉得在这个地方居住也很难集中心思读书，便再次搬

qiān dào chéng dōng jū zhù
迁到城东居住。

This time in the east of the city there was a schoolyard, where children always read books. Mencius started to imitate the others to sit down and study. This is how Mencius was able to become one of the most famous philosophers and thinkers after he grew up.

chéngdōng nà li yǒu ge xuétáng　jīngchángshūshēnglángláng　mèng zǐ guǒrán yě xuézhe qí tā rén de yàng zi
城 东那里有个学堂，经 常 书声 琅 琅 。孟 子果然也学着其他人的样子

zuòxià lái dú shū　　zhèngyīnwéi rú cǐ　mèng zǐ zhǎng dà xuéchéng yǐ hòu　cái chéngwéizhùmíng de zhéxué jiā hé
坐下来读书 。 正 因为如此，孟 子长 大学 成 以后，才 成 为著 名 的哲学家和

sī xiǎngjiā
思 想 家 。

 Shennong Tastes the Medicines

神农尝百草

〖Shennong Tastes the Medicines〗

A long long time ago, people often got ill, sometimes even died from eating unidentified food.   Shennong decided to taste everything.   Things that were regarded as food would be put into his left pocket,   and things that could be used as medicine went to his right pocket.

shén nóng cháng bǎi cǎo
神农 尝 百草

zài yuǎn gǔ shí hou   rén men jīng cháng yīn wéi luàn chī dōng xi ér shēng bìng   shèn zhì sàng mìng   shén nóng jué
在 远 古 时 候，人 们 经 常 因 为 乱 吃 东 西 而 生 病，甚 至 丧 命。 神 农 决

xīn cháng biàn suǒ yǒu de dōng xi   néng dāng shí wù de fàng zài zuǒ biān de dài zi lǐ   néng zuò yào yòng de jiù fàng zài
心 尝 遍 所 有 的 东 西，能 当 食 物 的 放 在 左 边 的 袋 子 里 ；能 作 药 用 的 就 放 在

shēn zi yòu biān de dài zi lǐ
身 子 右 边 的 袋 子 里。

The first thing Shennong tasted was a small leaf. This leaf was able to clean all his inner organs and made him feel fresh, like a little inspector, so Shennong called it "Cha", and later people gave it another name, as we all know, "tea". Shennong put it into his left pocket. The next thing he found was a small red flower that looked like a butterfly, with a sweet taste. Shennong called it "Gancao", meaning sweet grass. Shennong put it into his right pocket. Shennong tasted hundreds of plants, and everytime he got poisoned, he ate tea to cure himself. By the end Shennong's left pocket had 47 thousand types of food, and his right pocket had 398 thousand types of medicines.

第一次，神农尝了一片小叶子。这叶子可以把身体里面各器官清洗得清清爽爽，像一个巡查，神农把它叫作"查"，就是后人所称的"茶"。神农将它放进左边袋子里。第二次，神农尝了朵蝴蝶样的小红花，他感到小红花甜津津的，便称之为"甘草"，他把它放进了右边袋子里。就这样，神农辛苦地尝遍百草。每次中毒，都靠吃茶来解救。后来，他左边的袋子里食物有四万七千种，右边的药有三十九万八千种。

One day Shennong tasted "Duanchangcao", which was a strong poisonous grass that killed him before he could eat any tea. He sacrificed himself to save the people. People admired him as "the God of Chinese medicine", and remembered him ever since then.

dàn yǒu yì tiān   shénnóng cháng dào le   duàn cháng cǎo   zhè zhǒng dú cǎo shí zài tài lì hai   tā hái lái
但有一天，神农尝到了"断肠草"，这种毒草实在太厉害，他还来

bu jí chī chá jiě dú jiù sǐ le   tā shì wèi le zhěng jiù rénmen ér xī shēng de   hòurénmen chēng tā wéi   yào wáng
不及吃茶解毒就死了。他是为了拯救人们而牺牲的，后人们称他为"药王

pú sà   yǒngyuǎn de jì niàn tā
菩萨"，永远地纪念他。

 Pan Jinlian
潘金莲

〖Pan Jinlian〗

Pan Jinlian was a beautiful young woman with the grace of an eminent family, however, she was wrongly arranged to be married to an ugly dwarf named Wu Dalang. The couple lived in an apartment, owned by landlord Old Woman Wang.

One day, as Pan Jinlian was trying to shut the windows on the second floor with the help of a bamboo rod, it accidentally slipped from her hand and fell into the street, hitting a pedestrian on the head. He was the drugstore owner named Ximen Qing. Seeing that

pān jīn lián
潘金莲

潘金莲本是一个年轻美丽的富贵人家的女儿，后来阴差阳错地嫁给了又矮又丑的武大郎。夫妻二人住在一间小房子里面，房东是一个名叫王婆的老太太。

一天，潘金莲正在用一根竹子关二楼窗子的时候，不小心脱手，将竹子掉到街上，正好打在一个行人的头上。这人是一个药店老板，名叫

the culprit was a pretty woman, his anger immediately turned into luster. The dandy's gracious pardoning of her imprudence also left an indelible impression on Pan Jinlian.

Losing no time, Ximen Qing went into the teahouse owned by Old Woman Wang, who lived next door to Pan Jinlian. Pleased with his bribe, the money grubber old woman agreed to arrange a rendezvous between him and Jinlian.

西门庆。他本怒气冲冲，见到潘金莲的美貌，顿时起了色心。他大度地原谅了潘金莲，潘金莲心里对他也有了好感。

西门庆马上到隔壁王婆开的茶馆，请王婆安排二人见面。财迷心窍的王婆收了西门庆的贿赂，答应了他。

Old Woman Wang introduced Ximen Qing and Pan Jinlian to each other and left them alone. Brief and awkward greetings soon gave way to intimacy. They were in the middle of their affair when the old woman returned and caught them in action. Embarrassed and terrified, Pan Jinlian begged for mercy. Actually, this was part of the scheme to blackmail her into submission. Sure enough, when the Old Woman Wang threatened that she would tell her husband unless she agreed to come each time Ximen Qing wanted her, she agreed. Each morning, Pan Jinlian would be anxious to see her husband leave the apartment so that she could sneak into the next door.

王婆给潘金莲介绍了西门庆后，把二人单独留在屋子里。很快，刚见面时的尴尬和拘谨一扫而空，二人就在屋子里亲热起来。正在这时，王婆进屋来，跟他们撞个正着。潘金莲羞愧难当，苦苦恳求王婆开恩。其实这正是王婆精心设计地要挟她的手段。王婆告诉潘金莲，只要每次都顺从西门庆，就一定替她保密，潘金莲答应了。从那以后，每天早晨，潘金莲恨不得武大郎快点出去干活儿，好早点儿溜到隔壁去与西门庆约会。

Eventually, Wu Dalang's neighbors discovered the affair and told him about it. One day, he returned home early and went to the teahouse to confront the adulterous couple. Ximen Qing threw his leg and hit Wu Dalang hard on the chest. The nearly fatal injury confined him to bed. Instead of taking care of her husband, Pan Jinlian went to meet Ximen Qing as usual. The neglected and frustrated Wu Dalang threatened to tell everything to his brother Wu Song, who was a young officer, famous for killing a tiger once. To destroy the evidence, Ximen Qing plotted Wu Dalang's murder. Ximen Qing took a pouch of poison from his drugstore and gave it to Pan Jinlian. When Wu Dalang asked for medicine, Pan Jinlian adulterated the medicine with the poison.

不久，邻居们发现了二人的不轨行为，并告诉了武大郎。一天，武大郎早早回家，到茶馆去当场捉奸。西门庆见事情败露，飞起一脚，向武大郎胸口踢去，将他踢成重伤，卧床不起。这期间，潘金莲不但不照顾她丈夫，反而照旧每天去和西门庆相见。武大郎又急又怒，对潘金莲威胁，说要将此事告诉他的弟弟，打虎英雄武松。西门庆知道了，为了杀人灭口，设下一条毒计。他从药店配了烈性毒药，交给潘金莲。武大郎要喝药的时候，潘金莲将毒药掺进药里，给他灌了下去。

When Wu Song came and learned what had happened to his brother, he took the law into his own hands. Gathering a dozen neighbors as witness, he held a sentence of his own. He made Pan Jinlian and Old Women Wang confess in front of the witnesses and have their confessions documented, then he killed Pan Jinlian with his sword. When Wu Song found Ximen Qing in a restaurant, the two had a sword fight, but Ximen Qing was certainly not Wu Song's match. After only a few rounds, Wu Song threw him out of the restaurant's window and slain him with his sword.

武松得知此事，回来为哥哥报仇。他把邻居们都叫来，作为证人，当着大家的面逼着潘金莲和王婆招认了事情的经过。然后，武松一剑将潘金莲斩了。武松又在一个饭馆里找到了西门庆，两人挥剑比武，西门庆远远不是武松的对手。不几个回合，西门庆就被武松从窗子扔出去，又补上一剑，结果了他的性命。

Part III
Myths

第三部分
神话故事

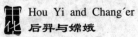 Hou Yi and Chang'er
后羿与嫦娥

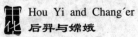 Hou Yi and Chang'er 后羿与嫦娥

《Hou Yi and Chang'er》

In the reign of the legendary emperor Yao, ten suns filled the sky. Their heat parched fields, wilted crops, and left people lying breathless and unconscious on the ground. Ferocious animals and birds fled boiling rivers and flaming forests to attack human beings. The immortals in heaven were moved by the people's suffering. The Emperor of Heaven sent the archer Hou Yi to help Yao bring order.

hòu yì yǔ cháng é
后羿与嫦娥

chuánshuō zài yáo de shí dài
传说在尧的时代，

yǒu shí ge tài yang tóng shí chū xiàn zài tiān kōng
有十个太阳同时出现在天空，

bǎ tǔ dì kǎo jiāo le
把土地烤焦了，

bǎ zhuāng jia dōu kǎo gān le
把庄稼都烤干了，

rén men rè de chuǎn bú guò qì lái
人们热得喘不过气来，

hūn dǎo zài dì shang
昏倒在地上。

yīn wéi tiān qì kù rè
因为天气酷热

nán dāng
难当，

yī xiē guài qín měng shòu
一些怪禽猛兽，

yě dōu cóng gān hé de jiāng hú hé huǒ yàn shì de sēn lín lǐ pǎo chū lái
也都从干涸的江湖和火焰似的森林里跑出来，

zài
在

gè dì cán hài rén mín
各地残害人民。

rén jiān de zāi nàn jīng dòng le tiān shang de shén
人间的灾难惊动了天上的神，

tiān dì mìng lìng shàn yú shè jiàn de hòu
天帝命令善于射箭的后

yì xià dào rén jiān
羿下到人间，

xié zhù yáo jiě chú rén mín de kǔ nàn
协助尧解除人民的苦难。

Hou Yi, with his beautiful wife Chang'er , descended to earth, carrying a red bow and white arrows given him by the Emperor of Heaven. People greeted the archer joyfully as a hero who might save them from their torment. Ready for battle, Hou Yi stood in the centre of the square, drew his bow and arrows, and took aim at the imperious suns. In an instant, one after the other, nine suns were shot from the sky. As Hou Yi took aim at the tenth, Yao stopped him - for the last sun might be of benefit to people. But Hou Yi had aroused jealousy of the other immortals, who slandered him before the Emperor of Heaven.

后羿带着天帝赐给他的一张红色的弓和一口袋白色的箭，携着美丽的妻子嫦娥一起来到人间。人们快乐地为射手欢呼，因为这位英雄可以帮助他们解除苦难。后羿立即开始了射日的战斗准备，他站在广场中央，从肩上拿下弓，取出箭，一支一支地向骄横的太阳射去，顷刻间十个太阳被射去了九个。正当后羿对准第十个太阳准备拉弓时，尧阻止了他，因为尧认为留下一个太阳对人民有用处。可是后羿后来却遭到了其他天神的妒忌，他们到天帝那里去进谗言。

Soon the archer sensed an aloofness and a lack of confidence in the Emperor's attitude. Finally, Hou Yi and his wife were banished forever from heaven and forced to live by hunting on earth. Hou Yi, sorry that his wife had to lead a mortal's life for his sake, obtained an elixir of immortality from Xiwangmu, the Queen Mother of the West. He hoped that, even though condemned to earth, he and his wife could live together happily and forever. Chang'er, however, resented her new hard life, and while Hou Yi was away from home, she swallowed all the elixir and flew to the moon.

hòu yì gǎn dào le tiān dì de shū yuǎn hé lěng luò　zuì hòu tiān dì xià lìng bǎ tā hé qī zi yǒng yuǎn biǎn chì
后羿感到了天帝的疏远和冷落。最后天帝下令把他和妻子永远贬斥

dào rén jiān　hòu yì hé qī zi cháng é bèi pò lái dào rén jiān　kào hòu yì dǎ liè wéi shēng　hòu yì jué de duì bu
到人间。后羿和妻子嫦娥被迫来到人间，靠后羿打猎为生。后羿觉得对不

qǐ shòu tā lián lěi ér zhé jū xià fán de qī zi　biàn dào xī wáng mǔ nà li qù qiú lái le cháng shēng bù lǎo zhī
起受他连累而谪居下凡的妻子，便到西王母那里去求来了长生不老之

yào　hǎo ràng tā men fū qī èr rén zài shì jiān yǒng yuǎn hé xié de shēng huó xià qù　cháng é què guò bú guàn qīng
药，好让他们夫妻二人在世间永远和谐地生活下去。嫦娥却过不惯清

kǔ de shēng huó　chéng hòu yì bú zài jiā de shí hou　tōu chī le quán bù de cháng shēng bù lǎo yào　táo bèn dào
苦的生活，乘后羿不在家的时候，偷吃了全部的长生不老药，逃奔到

yuè liàng lǐ qù le
月亮里去了。

 Kua Fu Chased the Sun

夸父追日

〖Kua Fu Chased the Sun〗

In antiquity a giant named KuaFu determined to have a race with the Sun and catch up with it. So he rushed in the direction of the Sun. Finally, he almost caught up to the Sun, but he was too thirsty and hot to continue. He swooped upon the Yellow River and Wei River earnestly and drank all the water in both rivers. But he still felt thirsty and hot, thereupon, he marched northward for the great lakes in the north of China. Unfortunately, he fell down and died halfway because of thirst. His cane dropped down as he fell, then the cane became a stretch of peach, green and lush.

kuā fù zhuī rì
夸父追日

传说古时有一个巨人，名叫夸父。 有一天，夸父决定要去和太阳赛跑，将太阳追上。于是他朝着太阳的方向奔去。 终于，他快要赶上太阳了。 突然间夸父感到实在是太渴、太热，跑不动了。于是，他跑到黄河和渭河两条大河去喝水，喝干了两条大河的水。可是，他仍然是又渴又热。因此，他朝着北方的大湖跑去。 很不幸，他最终倒在半路上，渴死了。 结果他手里的拐杖落在地下，变成了一片茂密的桃树林。

 Nv Wa Saves the Sky
女娲补天

〖**Nv Wa Saves the Sky**〗

Chinese legend has it that in remote antiquity there were no humans when a god called Pan Gu broke the chaotic universe and split the heaven and earth apart. This legend story came afterwards.

The god of water named Gong Gong and the god of fire named Zhu Rong had a fight. In the end Zhu Rong won, and Gong Gong was defeated.

nǚ wā bǔ tiān
女娲补天

zài yuǎn gǔ shí dài　tiān shén pán gǔ dǎ pò le　yǔ zhòu de hùn dùn zhuàng tài　kāi tiān pì dì　nà shí hái méi yǒu
在远古时代，天神盘古打破了宇宙的混沌 状 态，开天辟地。那时还没有

rén lèi ne　　ér hòu biàn yǒu le xià mian de chuán shuō
人类呢。而后便有了下面的传说。

shuǐ shén gòng gōng hé huǒ shén zhù róng nào fān le　　dǎ le qǐ lái　　zuì hòu zhù róng dǎ bài le gòng gōng
水神共工和火神祝融闹翻了，打了起来。最后祝融打败了共工。

Gong Gong was angry. He bumped into the Buzhou Mountain. The Buzhou Mountain stood as a pole in-between Heaven and Earth. When Buzhou Mountain fell, heaven was broken and a hole appeared in the sky. Nv Wa, the goddess, was very sad as she saw this happening.

gònggōng hěn fèn nù   cháo xī fāng de bù zhōushān zhuàng qù   nǎ zhī dào   bù zhōushān shì chēng tiān de zhù
共 工 很 愤怒 ， 朝 西方 的 不 周 山 撞 去，哪知道，不 周 山 是 撑 天的柱

zi   bù zhōushān dǎo le   yě jiù shì zhī chēng tiān dì zhī jiān de dà zhù zi duàn le   tiān chū xiàn le yí gè dà kū
子 。不 周 山 倒了 ，也就是支 撑 天地之间的大柱子 断了 ，天出 现了一个大窟

long   nǚ shén nǚ wā mù dǔ zhè yí qiè   xīn li fēi cháng nán guò
窿 。女 神 女娲目睹这一切 ，心里非 常 难过。

To save human kind from such disaster, she melted some five colored stones and patched up the sky. Then she cut off the four legs from a giant turtle to use them as new poles to hold up heaven and keep it from falling down.

Thus people lived peacefully ever after. Nv Wa is now known as the first heroine in Chinese history.

wèi le zhěng jiù rén lèi   shǐ tā men miǎn chú miàn lín de zāi nàn
为 了 拯 救 人类 , 使他们 免 除 面 临 的 灾难 。

nǔ wā xuǎn yòng gè zhǒng gè yàng de wǔ zhǒng
女娲 选 用 各 种 各 样 的 五 种

yán sè de shí zǐ   jià qǐ huǒ jiāng tā men róng huà chéng jiāng   yòng zhè zhǒng shí jiāng jiāng cán quē de tiān kū lóng tián
颜色的石子 , 架起火 将 它们 熔 化 成 浆 , 用这 种 石浆 将 残缺的天窟窿 填

hǎo   suí hòu nǔ wā yòu zhǎn xià yì zhī dà wū guī de sì zhī jiǎo   dāng zuò sì gēn zhù zi bǎ tiān zhī qǐ lái   yǐ miǎn
好 。 随后女娲又斩下一只大乌龟的四只脚 , 当作四根柱子把天支起来 , 以免

dǎo tā
倒塌 。

rén mín yòu chóng xīn guò zhe ān lè de shēng huó   nǔ wā bèi rén chēng wéi zhōng guó lì shǐ shang dì yī wèi nǔ yīng
人民又 重 新过着安乐的 生 活 。 女娲被人 称 为 中 国历史 上 第一位女英

xióng
雄 。

Lady White Snake
白蛇传

〚Lady White Snake〛

This legend story happened in the Song Dynasty. A white snake and a green snake, both of whom had magical power, transformed into two beautiful young ladies, one white, one green. One day they met a man named Xu Xian at the West Lake of HangZhou city. The white snake fell in love with Xu Xian at first sight. They got married soon after. The Lady White helped her husband to open a herbal medicine store by writing the prescriptions. Patients unable to pay were given free treatment and medicine. The store quickly became well known and popular.

báishézhuàn

白蛇 传

故事发生在宋朝。修炼成精的白蛇和青蛇化作两个美女，一个身着白色，一个身着青色。一天，她们在杭州的西湖边遇到一个名字叫许仙的男子。白蛇对许仙一见钟情。不久，两人喜结良缘。婚后，白蛇帮助丈夫开了一个中药铺，并亲自负责给病人开药方。对没有钱看病的穷人，他们经常免费送医送药。这件事很快就传开了。

One day a monk called Fa Hai traveled across Hang Zhou. He saw the couple and warned Xu Xian that his wife was a white snake. It was during the Dragon Boat Festival, when Chinese families like to decorate with reed and moxa around the house and drink wine to drive away spirits. This was dangerous to Lady White and Lady Green, since they were spirits after all. Lady White tried to drink wine to please her husband. Unfortunately, she couldn't control herself and turned into her snake body in her bedroom. Shocked from what he saw, Xu Xian passed out.

In order to save her husband's life, Lady White went to steal the resurrection plant on the Kunlun Mountain. Xu Xian's life was restored from the plant. However, he re-

有一天一个叫法海的和尚来到杭州。他看到许仙和白娘子后，警告

许仙说白娘子是一条白蛇。而那时正赶上龙船节。中国人家家户户

都用芦苇和艾蒿装点房门，并且要喝黄酒驱鬼。这对白蛇和青蛇来说

是十分危险的事情，因为她们的确也是精灵变化的。白蛇试着喝点黄酒

令许仙高兴，非常不幸的是白蛇没能控制住自己，在卧室里现出了蛇

身。许仙被吓得昏了过去。

为了救丈夫的命，白娘子去昆仑山盗来了还魂仙草。许仙得救

membered what Fa Hai told him and went to the Golden Mountain Temple to see him. Fa Hai suggested Xu Xian become a monk to forget his wife.   Lady White asked a great army of underwater creatures for help and brought forth a flood over the Golden Mountain Temple to fight with Fa Hai, but Fa Hai had more magical power and asked the heavenly soldiers to save his temple. Since the Lady White was pregnant, she was too weak to fight harder.   She gave up the battle and waited for the time after giving birth.   Fa Hai came and imprisoned the Lady White inside the Thunder Pagoda.

After the son of Lady White grew up, he and Lady Green fought back together, took revenge by destroying the Thunder Pagoda and rescued Lady White.   Lady White eventually reunited with her husband and her son.

后，仍记得法海的话，去金山寺看他。法海劝说许仙出家，忘掉凡尘。

白娘子求助于水里的虾兵蟹将，水漫金山，与法海大战一场。然而，

法海的道行更胜一筹，他请求天兵天将拯救寺庙。由于白蛇身怀有

孕，身体虚弱，无法恋战，因而败退下来。她要等到生产之后再与法海

一决高低。后来，法海将白娘子压在雷峰塔下。

白娘子的儿子长大以后，与小青一起来报仇。他们劈毁了雷峰塔，

救出了白娘子。白娘子终于与丈夫和儿子团聚在一起。

The Magic Goose
神鹅

中国传统文化经典故事100篇·英汉对照

〚The Magic Goose〛

Once upon a time, a giant goose came down to earth from the heavens, eating people and animals. To prevent further disasters, people sent brave warriors and killed the goose.

shén é
神鹅

hěn jiǔ hěn jiǔ yǐ qián　　 yǒu yì zhī dà é cóng tiān ér jiàng　 tā féng rén chī rén　féng chù chī chù　 wèi le bì
很久很久以前，有一只大鹅从天而降，它逢人吃人，逢畜吃畜。为了避

miǎn gèng dà de zāi nàn　　rén men pài chū yǒng shì　　jiāng zhè zhī é shā sǐ
免更大的灾难，人们派出勇士，将这只鹅杀死。

Although the Jade Emperor was usually an even tempered monarch, he got very angry when he heard about the magic goose's death, and decided to burn the world down on the 15th day of the 1st lunar month.

虽然玉皇大帝性格很温和，可是当他听说神鹅被凡人射死，仍然非常生气。他决定要于正月十五日晚上将人间全部烧尽。

中国传统文化经典故事100篇·英汉对照

A maid in the Jade Emperor's palace heard about this and hurried down to the earth to warn people. The palace maid also told people to raise lanterns and put up fires on that day, so that the world would look as though it were burning. When the heaven soldiers came down to carry out their mission, they got confused at seeing that the world was already burning, and went back to the heavens.

This is the origin of the Lantern Festival on the 15th day of the 1st lunar month

这件事被玉帝座前一位侍女知道了。她匆匆来到人间，警告人们要多加防范，并告诉大家在正月十五那天晚上家家户户要挂红灯笼，放烟火，好像整个人间已经着火一样。当天兵要下凡执行任务时，见火光一片，很是困惑不解，他们以为火已经烧起来了，回到天庭，向玉帝交差。

这就是农历正月十五灯笼节的来历。

Niu Lang and Zhi Nv

牛郎织女

〖Niu Lang and Zhi Nv〗

On the seventh day of the seventh lunar month, during the "Festival of the Seventh Evening", we remember the romantic legend story of a young couple, Niu Lang, "the Cowherd" and Zhi Nv, "the Weaving Maid".

Niu Lang was a handsome and hardworking boy. His parents died when he was young, and he lived with his older brother and his brother's wife, who were both very lazy and treated him as a servant.

牛郎织女

每到七夕节，农历的七月初七，我们就想起牛郎织女的浪漫传说。

牛郎是个英俊、勤劳的小伙子。他很小的时候父母都去世了，他只好跟着哥哥和嫂子过日子。牛郎的哥哥和嫂子都很懒惰，把他当成奴仆一样支使。

One day Zhi Nv from the heavens and her six sisters came to earth to bathe in a beautiful stream, where the Cowherd saw them and was transfixed by their beauty. When the sisters spotted him, six of them hurried to put on their clothes, turn into doves, and flew back to the realm of the Celestial Mother of the West. However, Zhi Nv's clothes were in Niu Lang's hand. As they talked, Zhi Nv fell in love with Niu Lang. She remained on the earth of mortals and married Niu Lang.

The young couple had two children, a boy and a girl, and lived happily together for some years. One day, the affair came to the attention of the Celestial Mother. She ordered her troops to abduct Zhi Nv and escort her back to her celestial loom. Their happy life had to be broken up.

一天，织女和她的六个姐妹从天上下凡，来到一条美丽的河里洗澡。牛郎恰巧看到她们，牛郎被仙女们的美丽惊呆了。众姐妹发现了牛郎，赶紧穿上衣服，变成鸽子飞回西天王母那里。然而，织女的衣服却被牛郎握在手里。他们说话时，织女看上了牛郎。织女留在了人间，嫁给了牛郎作妻子。

牛郎和织女结婚后，生活得很幸福，他们生了一男一女两个孩子，过了几年幸福而快乐的生活。但是好景不长，一天，王母娘娘知道了这件事，她命天兵天将，强行把织女带回天上织布，恩爱夫妻被拆散了。

With the help of a magic cow, Niu Lang took his children and went up to the heavens, to catch up with Zhi Nv. However, the Celestial Mother drew a hairpin from her hair, blew on it and turned it into a heavenly river, the one we know today as the Milky Way, and it flowed forth in between the couple, thus they were separated forever.

In recognition of their great love for each other, a flock of magpies miraculously appeared to form a bridge over the heavenly river. The Celestial Mother was eventually touched and allowed the lovers to be reunited on the magpie bridge for one night every year, on the 7th night of the 7th lunar month.

牛郎借助神牛的帮助，拉着自己的儿女，上天去追织女，眼见就要追到了，可是王母娘娘拔下头上的金簪一挥，一道天河就出现了，那就是我们今天所说的银河，牛郎和织女被永远地隔在两岸。

他们的忠贞爱情感动了喜鹊，成千上万只喜鹊飞来，在银河的上面搭成鹊桥。王母娘娘终于被感动了，她允许牛郎织女两人在每年七月七日在鹊桥相会。

 Liang Shanbo and Zhu Yingtai
梁山伯与祝英台

中国传统文化经典故事100篇·英汉对照

Long long ago there was a landlord surnamed Zhu. He had a daughter named Zhu Yingtai who was very beautiful and smart and enjoyed learning very much. However, the girl was not permitted to go to school during the old times, so she had to stay at home and looked at the students coming and going on the street through the window everyday. She envied them very much and thought: "Why does the girl have to stay at home and do the embroidering? Why can't I go to school?"

liáng shān bó yǔ zhù yīng tái
梁 山 伯 与 祝 英 台

从 前 有 个 姓 祝 的 地 主 ， 他 的 女 儿 祝 英 台 不 仅 美 丽 大 方 ， 而 且 非 常 聪 明 好 学 。 但 由 于 古 时 候 女 子 不 能 进 学 堂 读 书 ， 祝 英 台 只 好 每 天 倚 在 窗 栏 上 ， 望 着 街 上 来 来 往 往 的 读 书 人 ， 心 里 羡 慕 极 了 ， 心 想 ： "为 什 么 女 子 只 能 在 家 里 绣 花 ？ 为 什 么 我 不 能 去 上 学 ？ "

319

Suddenly she went back to the room and told her parents with courage: "Dad, Mom, I want to go to Hangzhou to have classes. I can wear a man's garments and act like a man and I will not be recognized. I promise. Please let me go, please!" The old couple didn't agree at first, but as Yingtai kept begging them, they agreed. The next morning, Yingtai and her maid, both in men's suits, set out to Hangzhou happily after saying farewell to her parents.

祝英台转身回到房间，鼓起勇气向父母要求："爹，娘，我要到杭州去读书。我可以穿男人的衣服，扮成男人的样子，一定不让别人认出来，我保证，你们就答应我吧！"老两口开始不同意，但经不住英台撒娇哀求，只好答应了。第二天一清早，天刚蒙蒙亮，祝英台就和丫鬟扮成男装，辞别父母，兴高采烈地出发去杭州了。

At school she met a classmate named Liang Shanbo, who was a knowledgeable young man with a great personality. They felt like old friends from the moment they saw each other for the first sight. The two talked and spent a lot of time together from then on. Later, they decided to be sworn brothers and became even more intimate.

Spring went and autumn came. Three years had passed. It was time to say goodbye to her teacher and return home. Zhu Yingtai felt she loved Liang Shanbo very much after three years of studying together. Liang also hated seeing her going home although he didn't know that she was a girl. They missed each other day and night after they arrived

dào le xuétáng de dì yī tiān　zhùyīngtái yù jiàn le yí gè jiào liángshān bó de tóngchuāng　liángshān bó xué
到了学堂的第一天，祝英台遇见了一个叫梁山伯的同窗，梁山伯学

shí yuān bó　wēnwén ěr yǎ　liǎngrénhěntóuyuán　yǒu yí zhòng yí jiàn rú gù de gǎnjué　yú shì　tā men
识渊博，温文而雅，两人很投缘，有一种一见如故的感觉。于是，他们

chángcháng yì qǐ liáotiān　hù xiāngguānxīn tǐ tiē　hòu lái　liǎngrén jié bài wéixiōng dì　guān xi gèng jiā mì
常常一起聊天，互相关心体贴。后来，两人结拜为兄弟，关系更加密

qiè
切。

chūn qù qiū lái　yí huàngsānniánguò qù le　xuénián qī mǎn　gāi shì cí bié lǎoshī　fǎnhuí jiā xiāng de
春去秋来，一晃三年过去了，学年期满，该是辞别老师，返回家乡的

shí hou le　tóngchuāngzhěngsānnián　zhùyīngtái yǐ jīngshēnshēn ài shang le tā de liángxiōng　ér liángshān bó
时候了。同窗整三年，祝英台已经深深爱上了她的梁兄，而梁山伯

suī bù zhī zhùyīngtái shì nǚ shēng　dàn yǔ tā fēnshǒu yě shí fēn de bù qíngyuàn　huí dào jiā hòu　tā liǎng er dōu
虽不知祝英台是女生，但与她分手也十分地不情愿。回到家后，他俩儿都

home. Several months later, Liang Shanbo went to visit Zhu Yingtai. To his surprise, he found that Yingtai was a beautiful young girl.

Later, Liang Shanbo sent a woman matchmaker to Zhu's to get the permission of marrying Yingtai. But the Landlord Zhu had already accepted the proposal of the young master surnamed Ma with a rich family background. Liang Shanbo felt utterly sad and got sick. Soon he died.

Yingtai, who opposed her father's decision of marrying her with Master Ma, became strangely silent when she received the message of her brother Liang's passing away. She put the red wedding apparel on and went into the bridle sedan. When the party

日夜思念着对方。几个月后，梁山伯前往祝家拜访，发现祝英台竟是一位年轻美貌的姑娘，令他又惊又喜。

此后，梁山伯请人到祝家去求亲。可祝老爷早已把女儿许配给了有钱人家的少爷马公子。梁山伯顿觉万念俱灰，一病不起，没多久就死去了。

听到梁山伯去世的消息，一直在与父母抗争反对包办婚姻的祝英台反而突然变得异常镇静。她套上红衣红裙，走进了迎亲的花轿。当迎亲

escorting the bride passed by the tomb of Liang Shanbo, there came a strong gust of wind. The party had to stop. Yingtai came out from the sedan and put the red wedding apparel off, revealing her white mourning dress. She cried loudly and sadly in front of the tomb. A sudden thunder-storm came and the tomb split with loud noise amazingly. Yingtai smiled, and jumped into the tomb before others could realize what was happening. Then the tomb closed with a loud noise again. The wind ceased and the cloud scattered. Two beautiful butterflies flew out of the tomb, dancing elegantly, freely and happily in the sun.

队伍路过梁山伯的坟前时，忽然间一阵飞沙走石，花轿不得不停了下来。只见祝英台走出轿来，脱去红装，露出一身白素服。她在坟前放声大哭，霎时间电闪雷鸣，"轰"的一声，坟墓裂开了一个大缝，众人还没反应过来，祝英台已微笑着纵身跳了进去。接着又是一声巨响，坟墓合上了。这时风消云散，雨过天晴，一对美丽的蝴蝶从坟里面飞出来，在阳光下自由地翩翩起舞。

 Zhong Kui Seizes the Demon

钟馗捉鬼

〚Zhong Kui Seizes the Demon〛

Emperor Xuanzong of the Tang Dynasty is famed for his beautiful concubine, Yang Guifei. He was so utterly infatuated with her that he eventually allowed the empire to fall into the hands of her protege, the rebel An Lushan. In the end, a coalition of the emperor's own soldiers forced him to order to hang herself, after which he abdicated and retired to mourn her.

His imperial ranks were traveling in the vicinity of Mount Li in Shanxi province when he came down with a severe illness and his temperature fluctuated wildly, and the

zhōng kuí zhuō guǐ

钟 馗 捉 鬼

唐玄宗因其美丽的妃子杨贵妃而闻名 。他对杨贵妃如此的迷恋以至最终把江山社稷败在她的干儿子，叛贼安禄山的手中 。 最后，士兵们联合起来迫使他下令让杨贵妃自刎 。此后唐玄宗退位，每天沉浸于对杨贵妃的悼念情怀之中 。

皇家队伍经过山西省丽山附近时，唐玄宗病倒了，发起了高烧， 队

ranks had to be stopped to allow him to recover. In a delirious slumber, he dreamt he was visited by a small demon. It wore a red skirt and had a great shoe on one foot while the other was naked. It came in and stole the scented bag belonging to the concubine Yang Guifei and a jade flute, and then scampered off. Shortly thereafter, in came a much larger demon, with a long blue robe and a black hat, who chased after the smaller demon, caught him and ate him. He turned and looked at the emperor. "Who are you?" asked emperor Xuanzong. "I am Zhong Kui. Although I rose to the academic rank of a state doctorate, but I was too ugly to be appointed and had no opportunity to serve the government of the living. However, now I serve the Jade Emperor by exorcizing demons."

伍不得不停下来将息。在神智模糊的昏睡中，他梦见一个小鬼参见。小鬼穿着红裙子，一只脚穿着一只大鞋，另一只脚光着。他进来偷走了杨贵妃的香囊和玉笛，然后逃走了。一会儿，又进来一个非常大的鬼，穿着蓝色长袍，戴着黑色帽子。他追上小鬼，逮住他，并将他吃掉。他转过身来看着皇上。"你是谁？"玄宗问。"我是钟馗。虽然我考取了进士，却因长得太丑陋，被取消了功名，因而没有机会效忠朝廷。不过，我现在效忠玉帝，为其驱鬼。"

When the emperor awoke, his fever had vanished, and he was well again, so he knew that his illness had been caused by the small demon that Zhong Kui had destroyed.

He told his dream to the court painter, Wu Daozi, who painted the scene. This painting, called "Zhong Kui Seizes the Demon" or simply "Zhong Kui Picture" has been reproduced in paintings and prints ever since then.

huáng dì xǐng hòu　shāo jiù tuì le　tā yǐ huī fù guò lái　tā rèn wéi tā de bìng shì xiǎo guǐ yǐn qǐ de　shì
皇 帝 醒 后 , 烧 就 退 了 , 他 已 恢 复 过 来 。 他 认 为 他 的 病 是 小 鬼 引 起 的 , 是

zhōng kuí qū chú de
钟 馗 驱 除 的 。

tā jiāng zì jǐ de mèng gào su gōng tíng huà shī wú dào zǐ　wú dào zǐ huà chū le tā miáo shù de qíng jǐng　zhè
他 将 自 己 的 梦 告 诉 宫 廷 画 师 吴 道 子 , 吴 道 子 画 出 了 他 描 述 的 情 景 。 这

fú huà jiào　zhōng kuí zhuō guǐ　huò jiǎn chēng　zhōng kuí tú　cóng nà shí qǐ biàn bú duàn de bèi lín mó yǔ fān
幅 画 叫 " 钟 馗 捉 鬼 " 或 简 称 " 钟 馗 图 " , 从 那 时 起 便 不 断 地 被 临 摹 与 翻

yìn　zài shì shang liú chuán kāi lái
印 , 在 世 上 流 传 开 来 。

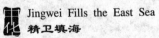

Jingwei Fills the East Sea
精卫填海

〔Jingwei Fills the East Sea〕

On Fajiu Hill grew a lot of mulberry trees. Among them lived a bird which looked like a crow, but had a colourful head, a white bill and two red claws. Its call sounded like its name: Jingwei. The bird was said to be Emperor Yandi's youngest daughter, who, while playing on the East Sea, had been drowned and never returned. She had turned into Jingwei, and the bird would often carry bits of twigs and stones all the way from the West Mountains to the East Sea to fill it up.

jīng wèi tián hǎi
精卫填海

fā jiū shānshangzhǎng le hěnduōsāngshù yǒu yì zhòngniǎo tā de xíngzhuàngxiàngwū yā tóu bù yǒuhuā
发鸠山 上 长 了很多桑树。有一 种 鸟，它的形 状 像乌鸦，头部有花

wén bái sè de huì hóng sè de jiǎo míngjiàojīngwèi tā de jiàoshēngxiàngzài hū huàn zì jǐ de míng zi
纹，白色的喙，红色的脚，名 叫精卫。它的叫 声 像在呼 唤自己的名字。

chuánshuōzhèzhǒngniǎoshì yán dì xiǎo nǚ ér de huàshēn yǒu yí cì tā qù dōnghǎiyóuyǒng bèi nì sǐ le
传 说这 种 鸟是炎帝小女儿的化身 。有一次，她去东海游泳，被溺死了，

zài yě méiyǒuhuí lái tā yǐ huàwéijīngwèiniǎo jīngchángkǒuxián xī shānshang de shùzhī hé shí kuài yòng lái
再也没有回来。她已化为精卫鸟，经 常 口衔西山 上 的树枝和石块，用来

tiándōnghǎi
填东海。

The Painted Skin
画皮

[The Painted Skin]

Once upon a time, a young man named Wang Sheng met a woman on the street. She was very beautiful, 16 years old. She told Wang Sheng that her husband beat her, so she ran away from home, and had no place to stay. Attracted by her appearance, Wang Sheng invited her to stay at his place. Wang Sheng's wife, Chen, begged him to let the woman go, but he didn't listen.

huà pí
画皮

古时候，有一个叫王生的人，一次在街上遇到一位女子，年芳十六，美艳绝代。她自称被丈夫毒打，逃了出来，无处容身。王生贪恋她的美色，将她接回家中，跟她同居一起。王生的妻子陈氏哀求丈夫，尽早把她送走，可是王生却听不进去。

One morning, Wang Sheng was taking a walk in the market when a Taoist priest came up and told him that he was surrounded by evil. Wang Sheng didn't believe him. He went home, and saw that the door was locked, so he went to the window and looked through. He saw a ferocious ghost, using a paint brush to draw on a piece of skin. After the ghost was finished, she put the skin onto her body, and turned into the beautiful woman.

有一天早晨，在集市上，王生撞见了一位道士。这位道士一见到他，就说："你的全身上下都被邪气围绕，定是遇到了妖精。"王生不信。走到了家门口时，只见大门紧紧地反锁着。他摸到窗户边，往里一看，只见一个面目狰狞的厉鬼坐在屋子里，她操起一支彩笔，往一张人皮上画着，画好了之后，往身上一披，立刻就变成了一位美女。

Wang Sheng was horrified. He ran back to the market and begged the priest for help. The priest then gave him a duster, told him to hang it onto the door for protection. After going home, the ghost saw the duster, and became very mad. She broke the duster, went to Wang Sheng's bed, and snatched his heart away.

chuāng wài de wángshēng zǎo yǐ xià de hún fēi pò sàn　　pǎo huí jí shì shang　　zhǎodào le dàoshi　　dà hǎn
窗 外的 王 生 早已吓得魂飞魄散，跑回集市上 ， 找到了道士， 大喊

jiù mìng　　yú shì dàoshi jiù jiāo gěi wángshēng yì bǎ fú chén　　jiāodài tā huí qù zhī hòu　　bǎ tā guà dào fángjiān
救命 。于是道士就交给 王 生 一把拂尘， 交待他回去之后， 把它挂到 房间

de mén shang　　　nà ge lì guǐ wàngjian fú chén　　nù qì chōngchōng de bǎ tā zhéduàn　　chōng dào wángshēng
的门 上。 那个厉鬼望见拂尘，怒气冲 冲 地把它折断， 冲 到 王 生

de chuángshàng　　bǎ wángshēng de xīnzàng wā zǒu le
的 床 上 ，把 王 生 的心脏挖走了。

Chen was shocked and cried. Later she went to the market, found the Taoist priest. He angrily came to Wang Sheng's home, found the ghost and slaughtered her. Chen begged the priest to save her husband. The priest said, "Go to the market and find a beggar. He is a little strange but he can save your husband's life." Chen went to see the beggar. The beggar spit into his hand, and told Chen to eat his phlegm. Chen was humiliated, but still ate it, and felt that a hard chunk of something went down to her chest. The beggar went away.

王 生 的妻子陈氏惊得大哭 。 后来她找到了集市上 的道人 ，道人

震怒，来到 王 生 家中 ，寻到妖怪 ，将其打死 。陈氏又哀求道人 ，一定

要救活 王 生 。 道人说道："在集市当 中 ，有一个疯疯 颠 颠的乞丐 ，

他能救你的 丈 夫 。"陈氏找 到了那乞丐 ，他吐出唾液在手 上 ，举到陈

氏的嘴边 ，大喊道："吃了它！ " 陈氏 强 忍着吃了下去 ，只觉得痰吞进

胸 中 ，变 成 了硬硬的一大团 。乞丐扬 长 而去 。

At the funeral, Chen cried loud out, holding her husband's body. All of a sudden, she felt that the chunk in her chest started beating, jumped out, and fell into the opening on Wang Sheng's chest. It was a heart! The next morning, Wang Sheng came back to life again.

zàng lǐ shàng　chén shì bào zhù shī tǐ　tòng kū shī shēng　tū rán jiān　tā jué de hěn xiǎng ǒu tù
葬礼上，陈氏抱住尸体，痛哭失声。突然间，她觉得很想呕吐，

zhǐ jué de xiōng zhōng nà tuán yìng kuài　tū tū tū de tiào le chū lái　diào jìn le zhàng fu de xiōng táng zhōng
只觉得胸中那团硬块，突突突地跳了出来，掉进了丈夫的胸膛中。

jū rán shì yì kē xīn　dì èr tiān zǎo shang　wáng shēng huó le guò lái
居然是一颗心！第二天早上，王生活了过来。

中国传统文化经典故事100篇·英汉对照

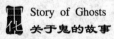

Story of Ghosts

关于鬼的故事

There are many stories of ghosts in Chinese culture. Ghosts have been believed by Chinese for a few thousand years. Even Confucius said, "Respect ghosts and gods, but stay away from them."

Zhuxi was a famous scholar in the Song Dynasty. He decided to write an essay titled, "No Ghost." When ghosts knew he was writing the essay, they gathered together to discuss this and decided to send the smartest ghost to entreat him to abandon the writing.

guān yú guǐ de gù shì
关于鬼的故事

中国文化中，有很多有关鬼的故事。数千年来很多中国人相信世上有鬼。连孔子都说："尊敬鬼神，但是远离它们。"

朱熹是宋朝的著名学者。一次他准备写一篇文章，标题是"无鬼论"。鬼听说他要写这篇文章，便聚在一起商量，决定派一个最聪明的鬼去恳求朱熹放弃这个念头。

第三部分 神话故事

337

So one night, the smartest ghost appeared at Zhuxi's desk. Zhuxi was surprised and asked,

"How dare you disturb me at night. "

"I have very important things to entreat you, sir."

Then the ghost begged Zhuxi to abandon the writing.   Zhuxi laughed and said, "Well, I heard you can do anything. Can you move me to the outside?"

"Certainly, sir."

yú shì yì tiān wǎnshàng   zhè ge cōngmíng de guǐ chūxiàn zài zhū xī de shūzhuōpáng   zhū xī hěn jīng yà
于是一天晚上，这个聪明的鬼出现在朱熹的书桌旁。 朱熹很惊讶，

wèndào
问道：

nǐ zěn gǎn zhè me wǎn lái dǎ rǎo wǒ
"你怎敢这么晚来打扰我？"

guǐ shuō   xiānsheng   wǒ yǒu zhòngyào de shì qiú nǐ
鬼说："先生，我有重要的事求你。"

guǐ qiú zhū xī bú yào xiě zhè piān wénzhāng   zhū xī xiào le   shuōdào   wǒ tīngshuō nǐ men shéntōng
鬼求朱熹不要写这篇文章。 朱熹笑了，说道："我听说你们神通

guǎng dà   nǐ néng bǎ wǒ cóng zhè lǐ yí dào wàimiàn qù ma
广大，你能把我从这里移到外面去吗？"

dāngrán kě yǐ   xiānsheng
"当然可以，先生。"

Zhuxi was moved to the outside instantly. Zhuxi was astonished by the ability of ghosts. He asked again, "You can move my body. Can you move my heart?"

"That is impossible to do, sir, we can only move things or a person's body so that it proves we exist. We exist in illusion. If you believe it, there will be, but if you don't, there will not."

Zhuxi felt the words did have some merit, so he wrote the little words, under the title of the "No Ghost" essay, "If you believe it, there will be, but if you don't, there will not."

于是朱熹立刻被移到屋子外面。 他很惊叹鬼的能力，又问道："你能

移动我的身体，但是你能移动我的心吗？ "

"这个我办不到，先生，我们只能移动物品或者人的身体，来证明

我们的存在。我们是存在于虚幻中的。如果你相信我们，就有鬼；如果你

不相信，就没有鬼。 "

朱熹觉得鬼的话很有些道理，于是在"无鬼论"标题的下面加上了一行

小字："信则有，不信则无"。

340

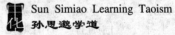
Sun Simiao Learning Taoism
孙思邈学道

〖Sun Simiao Learning Taoism〗

Sun Simiao was a native of Huayuan. At the age of seven he could recite many lines daily. When Dugu Xin met him, he signed: "What a child prodigy! It's a pity that he has too big an ambition to be put in an important post." When he grew up, he was fond of books written by Lao Zi and Zhuang Zi. It was an eventful period when Emperor Xuan of the Zhou Dynasty was in power. Sun Simiao separated himself in Taibai Mountain, learning Taoism and seeking the way of immortality.

sūn sī miǎoxuédào
孙思邈学道

孙思邈，华原人，七岁便能日诵千言，独孤信见了就感叹说："真是神童啊，可惜他心器太大，难以为用。"等到长大，他好读老子和庄子。周宣帝时，朝政多事，他隐居太白山学道，研究长生不老之术。

341

He was proficient in astronomy, astrology and medicine. Emperor Wen of the Sui Dynasty invited him to be the grand master of the state, but he declined it. Once he told others in private: "A holy man will be in power in fifty years and I'll go out of the mountain to succor the world and help the people." He didn't go to the capital until Emperor Taizhong of the Tang Dynasty sent an order. Emperor Taizhong was very surprised to find that he still looked young, saying: "I've heard before that Taoist practitioners should be respected. It's true that celestial beings will never age!"

孙思邈通晓天文星占，精于医药。隋文帝召他为国子博士，被他拒绝。

他曾私下对别人说："再过五十年，会有圣人当政，那时我才出山相助，济世救民。"等到唐太宗相召，他才进京。太宗见他容貌依然那么年轻，极为惊讶说："以前就听说得道之人值得尊重，神仙不老，此言不虚啊！"

In the third year of Yonghui, he had already been over one hundred years old. One day, having taken a bath and put on clean clothes, he said to his descendants: "Today I'll travel to an unknown place." After it, he passed away. A month had passed but his dead face was unchanged. Only his clothes were found when he was to be put into coffin.

yǒnghuī sān nián　　tā yǐ jīng yì bǎi duō suì le　　yì tiān mù yù hòu　chuān dài hǎo zhěng jié de yī guān　duì
永徽三年，他已经一百多岁了，一天沐浴后，穿戴好整洁的衣冠，对

zǐ sūn men shuō　　wǒ jīn rì jiāng yóu xū wú zhī xiāng le　　shuō wán qì jué　　guò le yí gè duō yuè　qí miàn
子孙们说："我今日将游虚无之乡了。"说完气绝。过了一个多月，其面

sè yī rán bú biàn　děng dào rù guān shí　zhǐ shèng xià kōng yī ér yǐ
色依然不变，等到入棺时，只剩下空衣而已。

 Zhuang Zi Refused to Be an Official
庄子不仕

〚Zhuang Zi Refused to Be an Official〛

Zhuang Zi, a native of the Meng County and named Zhuang Zhou, was once a senior official in the reign of King Hui of the Liang State and King Xuan of the Qi State. He studied all round knowledge, but his ideas were basically conformed to Lao Zi's. He did more than sixty thousand words of writing, most of which was in the form of allegory.

zhuāng zǐ bú shì
庄子不仕

zhuāng zǐ　méngxiànrén　míngzhuāngzhōu　céngzuòguò qī yuán lì　yǔ liánghuì wáng　qí xuān wáng
庄 子，蒙 县人，名 庄 周，曾做过漆园吏，与梁惠王，齐宣王

tóngshí dài　zài xué yè shang　tā wú suǒ bù kuī　dàn qí jī běn sī xiǎng yǔ lǎo zi xiāngtōng　tā zhùshū liù wàn
同时代。在学业上，他无所不窥，但其基本思想与老子相通。他著书六万

duō zì　dà dōushì yù yán tǐ
多字，大都是寓言体。

King Wei of the Chu State heard of his wisdom and sent a messenger to invite him with generous gifts and promise to appoint him the prime minister. Zhuang Zi smiled and said to the messenger: "It's said that there was a divinity turtle in the Chu State, which had been dead for three thousand years. The king put it into an elegant box wrapped with silk, which was then hidden in a temple.

楚威王听说庄子贤明多才,于是派使者带着厚礼去聘请他,许诺让他担任宰相。庄子笑着对使者说:"我听说楚国有一只神龟,已经死了三千年了,楚王把它用精美的盒子盛着,再用丝绸包着,藏在庙堂之中。

As far as this turtle is concerned, would it choose to be valuable after death or to wag its tail crawling in the mud while alive?" The messenger responded: "It will surely choose to wag the tail crawling in the mud while alive." Zhuang Zi then said: "That's right and that is also my choice." So he refused to be an official all his life and later he became immortal.

rán ér duì zhè zhī guī lái shuō
然而对这只龟来说，tā yuàn yì sǐ le bèi rén jìng zhòng ne 它愿意死了被人敬重呢？hái shì yuàn yì huó zhe tuō zhe wěi ba pá 还是愿意活着拖着尾巴爬

xíng yú làn ní zhōng ne
行于烂泥中呢？" shǐ zhě shuō 使者说："tā dāng rán huì xuǎn zé tuō zhe wěi ba zài làn ní lǐ pá xíng它当然会选择拖着尾巴在烂泥里爬行。"

zhuāng zǐ shuō
庄子说："duì对，nà yě zhèng shì wǒ de xuǎn zé那也正是我的选择。" yīn cǐ因此，tā zhōng shēn bù kěn wéi guān他终身不肯为官。hòu lái后来

zhuāng zǐ chéng le shén xiān
庄子成了神仙。

Ji Kang Met Ghosts

稽康会鬼

〖Ji Kang Met Ghosts〗

Ji Kang, alias Shuye, was a native of Zhi in the Qiao State. A man named Wang Botong built a guesthouse. Those who lodged there all died. The house had to be closed. But Ji Kang demanded staying there. He played a musical instrument to kill time. In the dead of night eight ghosts appeared. At first Ji Kang was fearful. He read the Book of Change silently to keep calm and then asked: "Have you killed those lodgers here before?" The ghosts answered: "No. We were musical players of Shun Danasty. We were eight brothers, and we were murdered by treacherous court officials and were buried

jī kāng huì guǐ
嵇康会鬼

嵇康，字叔夜，谯国人。有一个叫王伯通的人，建了一座馆舍。凡在那里寄宿的人都死了，于是王伯通只好将它关闭。而嵇康却要求在那里寄宿，他借弹琴消磨时光，午夜时分，果然出现了八个鬼。嵇康起初害怕，默诵《易经》镇定情绪，然后问道："以前在此寄宿的人都是为你们所杀吗？"鬼答："不是。我们是舜时的乐官，兄弟八人，因受奸臣谋害冤死，埋

here. Wang Botong built walls on our grave, which pressed us too much to tolerate. Whenever people came, we wanted to appeal to them. But to our surprise they were dead on seeing us. We had no intention of killing people. Hope you can inform Wang Botong. Ask him to rebury our skeletons. In half a year he will be the governor of the county. In order to express our thanks, we'll teach you a verse of Guangling." Happily Ji Kang gave his musical instrument to the ghosts, who played it once. Ji Kang learnt it in a moment. On the second day, he told the event to Wang Botong, who had the place dug and found the skeletons. Then he found a good place to bury them in coffins. Soon Emperor Wu of Jin was in power. As expected, Wang Botong was appointed the governor.

葬在此。 王伯通在我们的坟上筑墙，将我们压得无法忍受，见人来住，

我们就想申诉。不料，他们见了我们都吓死了，实在不是我们杀人。希望您

告诉王伯通，让他取出我们的骸骨另行埋葬。半年后他就可为本郡的太

守。今夜我们教您《广陵》一曲，聊表谢意。"稽康十分高兴，将琴递给

鬼，鬼弹了一遍，他马上就学会了。第二天，他将此事告诉王伯通。王伯

通派人挖掘，果然见到骸骨。他派人另外找了一个好地方将他们棺葬。不久

晋文帝即位，他果真如期当了太守。

Once Ji Kang roamed about the world with Sun Deng, who always kept silent and only when they parted he said: "Though you have talents, you are not good at protecting yourself." Just as expected, he was murdered. However according to Ji Zhuan Yuan Hai, Governor Bao Liang of Nanhai County used to be the master of Xu Ning in Donghai. Xu Ning heard very beautiful music from a quiet room, so he asked Bao Liang: "Who is playing?" Bao Liang answered: "It's Ji Kang." Xu Ning continued to ask: "Wasn't he killed in Dong City? How could he be here?" Bao Liang explained: "Though he was killed, he became immortal in fact."

jī kāng céng suí sūn dēng zhōu yóu shì jiè　　sūn dēng yì zhí guǎ yán shǎo yǔ　　zhí dào fēn shǒu shí　　tā cái duì jī
嵇康 曾 随孙登 周游世界，孙 登一直寡言少语。直到分手时，他才对嵇

kāng shuō　　　nǐ cái xué suī gāo　　dàn bú shàn yú zì bǎo　　　　guǒ rán hòu lái jī kāng bèi shā　　bú guò　　记纂
康 说："你才学虽高，但不善于自保。"果然后来嵇康被杀。不过《记纂

yuān hǎi　　lìng yǒu yì zhǒng shuō fǎ　　nán hǎi tài shǒu bào liàng　　céng wéi dōng hǎi xú níng de shī fù　　yī tiān yè
渊海》另有一种 说法："南海太守鲍靓，曾为东海徐宁的师傅。一天夜

wǎn xú níng tīng dào jìng shì zhōng yǒu qín shēng　　jí wéi měi miào　　yú shì wèn bào liàng　　shuí zài tán qín　　bào
晚徐宁听到净室 中有琴 声，极为美妙，于是问鲍靓："谁在弹琴？"鲍

liàng dá　　jī kāng　　xú níng yòu wèn　　jī kāng bú shì zài dōng shì bèi zhǎn le ma　　zěn me yòu zài zhè lǐ
靓答："嵇康。"徐宁又问："嵇康不是在东市被斩了吗？怎么又在这里

ne　　bào liàng jiě shì shuō　　jī kāng suī rán bèi zhǎn　　dàn shí jì shang chéng xiān le
呢？"鲍靓解释说："嵇康虽然被斩，但实际上 成 仙了。"

351

 Dongfang Shuo Escaped from the Outside World
东方朔避世

〖Dongfang Shuo Escaped from the Outside World〗

Dongfang Shuo, alias Manqian, was a native of Pingyuanyanci. In the reign of Emperor Wu of the Han Dynasty, he submitted a self-recommendation to offer his service to the Emperor. His words sounded arrogant and conceited, which made Emperor Wu regarded him as extraordinary. He was appointed a royal attendant in Gongcheshu and then in Jinmamen, and he often served in the royal palace. Once Emperor granted him some food, after the meal, he took all the leftover away, which made his clothes dirty. Many times when the Emperor granted silk to him, he would try to take as much as he could carry. He used all the rewards to marry Changan beauties. A marriage would last about a

东方朔避世

东方朔，字曼倩，平原厌次人。汉武帝时，他上书自荐，文辞不恭，自命不凡，武帝把他当成怪才看待，起初任公车署待诏，后又迁为金马门待诏。他得以经常在宫中侍奉。有一次皇上赐宴给他，吃完后，他把剩下的肉都揣在怀中带走，衣服也弄脏了。皇帝屡次赐给他丝帛，他都是肩担手提而去，用这些丝帛选娶长安美女。娶过来的美女一年左右

year before he married a new girl. All the granted money was spent on women. When he was laughed at, he said: "I am the very person who separates himself in the royal court to escape from the outside world." Once he drank so much that he sat on the ground, singing: "I separate myself among the mortal folks. I escape from outside but into the royal court. Why should one live in a mountain hut if he can be himself in the common world?"

jiù bèi tā pāo qì　tā yòu lìng qǔ xīn rén　shǎng cì dé lái de qián yě quán dōu huā zai nǚ rén shēn shang　bié rén cháo
就被他抛弃，他又另娶新人。赏赐得来的钱也全都花在女人身上。别人嘲

xiào tā　tā què shuō　wǒ jiù shì suǒ shuō de bì shì yú cháo tíng de rén　yǒu yí cì hē jiǔ xìng qǐ　tā zuò
笑他，他却说："我就是所说的避世于朝廷的人。"有一次喝酒兴起，他坐

zài dì shang chàng dào　wǒ chāo tuō zì jǐ yú sú rén zhī zhōng　wǒ bì shì yú huáng gōng jīn mǎ mén　yí gè rén
在地上唱道："我超脱自己于俗人之中，我避世于皇宫金马门，一个人

kě yǐ bì shì yú chén shì　yòu hé bì táo jìn shān lín máo wū zhī zhōng ne
可以避世于尘世，又何必逃进山林茅屋之中呢？"

Before his death, he said to his fellow official: "Nobody knows who I am except Lord Dawu." When Emperor Wu heard of it, he sent for Lord Dawu. When he couldn't give an answer, Emperor Wu asked him again: "What special ability do you have?" He replied: "All the stars are in the right place except for Jupiter, which had been out of sight for forty years, but came out recently." Looking up, Emperor Wu signed: "Dongfang Shuo had stayed beside me for eighteen years, but I never knew he was the embodiment of Jupiter." He was then in a bad mood.

东方朔临死前，对同舍的郎官说："天下了解我的底细的人只有大伍公。"后来，汉武帝听说了，召大伍公来问，大伍公回答不出来。武帝于是改问："您有什么特别的才能？"答："善于观察星相。"武帝问："所有的星宿都正常吗？"答："所有星宿都在正常的位置，只有木星消失了四十年，最近才重新出现。"武帝仰天叹道："东方朔在我身边十八年，我却不知道他是木星化身。"于是惨然不乐。